# REVELATIONS

K'WAN

CASH MONEY CONTENT

## Animal

First Trade Paperback Edition: November 2014

Book Layout: Jacquelynne Hudson

Cover Design: Baja Ukweli

www.CashMoneyContent.com

Library of Congress Control Number: 2014949040

ISBN: 978-1-936399-93-2 pbk
ISBN: 978-1-936399-94-9 ebook

10  9  8  7

Printed in the United States

# PROLOGUE

SOMEWHERE IN PUERTO RICO:

*"If you stop you're dead,"* were the words echoing in Chris's mind that kept him moving. His lungs burned, and his heart beat so hard in his chest that he felt like it might explode. His legs threatened to give out on him, but he knew if he stopped it would be over. If he could just make it to the harbor, he might still have a chance.

Chris heard a whistling sound and moved his head just as something whizzed by, nicking his cheek. He touched his fingers to his face and they came away bloody. Buried in the side of the building a few feet away was a dart. Hanging from the end of it was an orange tuft of fur. Chris spun, gun raised, eyes sweeping the dark street. Even though he couldn't see his pursuer, Chris knew he was close. His pursuer could've ended it blocks ago if he so chose, but he was toying with Chris, like a cat playing with a mouse before devouring it. Chris couldn't go out like this . . . not when he was so close.

Ignoring the cramping in his legs, Chris forced himself to

continue on. He cut down an alley that opened up on the next block. In this distance he could see the harbor. A friend of his was waiting for him with a boat to take him to safety. He was going to make it! As Chris ran he felt a burning sensation in his cheek where the dart had nicked him. The sensation spread throughout his face, and then crept into his chest. He felt like his lungs were constricting and he was finding it hard to draw breath. His sprint slowed to a jog, then finally an uncoordinated stagger. It was as if his legs and brain were no longer cooperating. At the mouth of the other end of the alley, so close to freedom, Chris's legs finally gave out and he fell to the ground.

Chris lay on the cold cobblestones, fighting to stay conscious. He could hear the sounds of footfalls nearing him, but had not the strength to lift his head. The footsteps stopped just short of where he was lying. A silhouette loomed over him. Chris fought against the fog that was trying to engulf his brain and forced his eyes to focus. He could make out a figure standing over him, wearing a dark cloak and hood that shadowed his face.

"What did you do to me?" Chris asked in a groggy voice.

"The dart was tipped with the poison of the Boxfish," the hooded figure said in a feminine voice, much to Chris's surprise. She knelt beside him, reaching to touch his neck to check his vitals. Chris could feel the cold from the steel-lined gauntlet she wore. It was then that he was able to catch a glimpse of what was hiding beneath the hood. Her face was covered by an ornately decorated mask, with a bright orange flower carved into the forehead. "Not as lethal as what I'd have normally used, but I didn't want it to kill you, just to keep you still for a few moments. Poisoning someone of your standing in these parts would raise too many questions. Your death will be attributed to being in the wrong place at the wrong time."

"You'll never get away with this. Do you know who my family is?" Chris asked in desperation.

"Indeed I do, and it is because of your family's standing on the island that I'm giving you the honor of a quick death," the masked female told him. There was the sound of compressed air being released and from the fingertips of her gauntlets sprouted razor sharp claws.

"My sister will see you dead for this. She'll track you to whatever holes you try to hide in, looking for payback!" Chris spat.

"That's exactly what I'm expecting to happen," she told him, before slashing his throat and leaving him to bleed out.

# BOUND BY BLOOD

ANIMAL STOOD ON THE BEACH LOOKING OUT at the water. The sun was just starting to set, casting a golden reflection across the surface of the rolling waves. He could stare at the Pacific Ocean for hours, and sometimes he would. There was something about it that made him feel at peace. Peace in his later years was exactly what Animal needed, considering how chaotic his entire life had been.

Animal spared a glance over his shoulder and took in the place he had called home since his release from prison. It was a far cry from the Harlem slum he had grown up in. It was a three-story house that sat mere yards from the beach, and there wasn't a neighbor for at least a mile. Located in the Latigo Shores section of Malibu and built to Animal's specifications, it was as secure as it was beautiful. Everyone privy to floor plans of Animal's haven had either died under mysterious circumstances or vanished without a trace. Though Animal wasn't in the *life* anymore, he only knew one way to keep a secret and old habits died hard. Between his reputation in the streets, and the very public spectacle of his violent life, Animal valued his privacy. After all he'd been through, he earned it.

Animal was a true product of his environment, one of the forgotten children of Harlem. His father took a walk and never came back when Animal was a toddler and his crack addict mother left him at the mercies of her boyfriend, who hated Animal's guts. To say that he had a hard childhood would've been an understatement. The abuses he was subject to were inhumane. Just shy of his thirteenth birthday, he'd decided he'd had enough and set out to tackle the world on his own. Life at home had been bad for him, but life on the streets was merciless. It was in the streets that he would receive his baptism by fire and earn the moniker *Animal*. He was a young savage who was willing to do whatever it took in the name of survival, including murder.

Growing up in chaos robbed Animal of ever having a real childhood and he had to become a man far sooner than other little boys his age. He learned very quickly that if he hoped to survive the jungle, he'd have to adapt to its rules and adapt he did. Animal had committed his first murder by the time he was fourteen and had swum a river of blood before he was old enough to vote. His psychological detachment from the rest of the world allowed Animal to do what others didn't have the stomach for and made him the perfect killer. He was on pace to die young and infamous, but love got in the way and changed things.

He'd met his future wife, Gucci, during one of the most turbulent periods in his life. Animal was heavy in the streets and the line of enemies and victims he had accounted for stretched for miles. The last thing he wanted to do was fall in love, but his heart had betrayed him and let her in. Animal was an expert at killing, but very much a novice when it came to dealing with the opposite sex. Gucci became his teacher, and Animal the willing student. Having Gucci in his life gave him balance; she helped him suppress the monster vying for control of his soul. She became his strength, but also his weakness, because it was his love for her that his enemies brought into play against him that led to his eventual downfall and eventual resurrection.

Animal and Gucci's adversities had been movie worthy, and would've likely destroyed most relationships, but it strengthened their bond. Even during their two-year separation, when Animal was a fugitive from justice, they still carried each other in their hearts. It was this intense love that sent Animal over the edge when word reached him that Gucci had been shot. The bullet hadn't been meant for her, but she was simply in the wrong place at the wrong time, but it didn't matter to Animal. They had touched the only thing in the world that he loved, and it was enough to send him on a killing spree that would make the five-o'clock news.

For his bleeding heart and violent temper, Animal was sentenced to a very lengthy prison sentence. He was supposed to never see the sun again, but Animal had one more trump card to play before they closed the curtains on him. Some very important people owed Animal some big favors and he called in every last marker. Eighteen months after he was sentenced, Animal was back on the streets with his lady. Some might've called it a miracle, but he called it blackmail. Animal had narrowly avoided the fate waiting for him, and it was after that he decided he'd had his fill of the streets. He was going to show his appreciation of his good fortune by focusing on his marriage and being a father. It had been easy to give his word to Gucci, but keeping it was proving to be a bit more complicated.

Having powerful people in his debt had provided Animal with the means to soften the blow the judicial system had tried to hit him with, but it still took money to pull the whole charade off. All total, Animal had spent nearly two million dollars greasing palms and making evidence disappear. He was doing very well financially, as a result of winning the lawsuit against Big Dawg Entertainment for back royalties from his posthumous album sales. Don B. figured that since Animal was supposed to be dead he could make the money go missing without anyone contesting it, but when Animal resurfaced it changed things. Don B. knew what kind of man Animal was so he settled out of court instead of fighting it and risking turning up dead. Animal had been awarded a nice sum, enough to set him and Gucci up in the house they were living in, and tuck a chunk away for a rainy day. But the money sacrificed getting him out of prison put a serious dent in his savings. Gucci knew that things were tight, but she had no idea how tight. They weren't broke, but an infusion of cash wouldn't hurt and there was only one way Animal knew to get it. When Animal was released he vowed to his wife that he was officially out, and his guns would bark no more, but he now found himself on the cusp of breaking that promise.

Animal felt them before he saw them. Their shadows were cast in the sand, growing as they drew closer to him. Animal turned his back to the rolling waves to face them, hands instinctively coming to rest on the two guns he had holstered to his sides. He wouldn't need them; it was more out of habit than feeling threatened by his visitors.

There were two of them, a woman and a young man. Her long black hair was pulled into a tight bun at the back of her head and her eyes were hidden by sunglasses, even though the sun was now fully set. A tight black bodysuit, hugged her like second skin, highlighting her toned legs and curvaceous hips. It was warm that night, yet she wore a black three-quarter jacket, buttoned to the neck with the belt drawn tightly around her waist. She took soft steps, barely leaving a print where her black boots touched the sand, and stopped a few feet shy of Animal. Her black painted lips curled slightly at the corners, in way of a greeting.

The young man trailed behind her. Unlike the woman, his steps were awkward and heavy. A few times he stumbled as if he would lose his footing, no doubt attributed to the heavy construction Timberlands he wore. The tops of the boots nearly touched the ends of his baggy jean shorts. In California, he stuck out like a sore thumb, as only New Yorkers would think to match shorts with boots. He now wore his hair in a short, nappy afro, and had began to sprout the first signs of a beard, but he still had a baby face. When he was finally able to steady himself, he looked over at Animal, flashing his best menacing scowl, tight eyes and barely a hint of teeth showing . . . just as Animal had taught him.

A few long moments passed with the three of them just staring at each other. It was as if it was a competition to see who could last the longest without breaking. They were all capable of playing the game for hours, but they didn't have that kind of time, so the young man broke the silence first.

"Fuck all this tough guy shit. What up, Blood?" the young man threw his arms open and stepped towards Animal.

Animal smiled and embraced his protégé. "Sup, Ashanti?" It felt good to see a familiar face after so long spent around strangers. He and Gucci had been living in California since his release from prison and it had been ages since he'd seen one of his old crime partners. Animal broke the embrace and held Ashanti at arm's length to look him over. Ashanti had put on about fifteen pounds of muscle since last time he'd seen him. "Damn, you're bigger than I remember. Fatima must be feeding your ass." He joked. Ashanti was no longer the skinny kid who used to follow him around the projects, begging him to put in work. He was a man now.

"Double F, feed me and fuck me. You know how it go, big homie," Ashanti laughed.

"I don't know if I'm surprised or disappointed that any woman would let you kiss them with that filthy mouth of yours. One day your tongue is going to fall out of that degenerate ass head of yours," the woman spoke up, not bothering to hide her disapproval with his language.

"I forgot the principal was with me on this class trip," Ashanti mumbled.

"Hardly. I have no desire to baby a grown ass man, but I will correct you when you're out of pocket. You asked me to show you the way and that's what I'm trying to do, but it isn't going to work if you fight me at every turn," Kahllah told him.

"C'mon, K, I'm just joking with the homie. Why are you so serious all the time?" Ashanti asked.

"Because there's no room for games in my life. If you want people to take you seriously and stop looking at you like a little ghetto bastard then I suggest you stop acting like one. Think before you speak, even if it's amongst family," she schooled him.

"When you're done giving your little lesson, can you show your brother some love?" Animal interjected.

Kahllah let her scolding eyes linger on Ashanti for a few seconds longer before shaking her head and turning to her brother. "Sorry," she embraced him. "How've you been?"

"Chilling, just enjoying my freedom, ya know?"

"No, I don't know because I've never been arrested," Kahllah said half jokingly.

"The ever elusive Black Lotus," Animal winked. "You're making quite the name for yourself in the streets."

"And how would you know, being that you spend most of your time out here with the rest of the rich folks?" she teased him.

"Sis, you know no matter where I lay my head, my ear is always to the curb. How are things with the Brotherhood?" he asked, referring to the Brotherhood of Blood.

The Brotherhood, as they were referred to, were a fraternal order of assassins, rumored to be founded sometime in the late eighteen hundreds. The dark hand of the Brotherhood was said to have orchestrated some extremely high profile assassinations, but it was hard to pen a murder on a phantom. The Brotherhood were ghost to all except their members, which included Kahllah. She was one of only three females ever inducted into their order, and the first to ever earn a seat at the big boy table.

"Bad," she said with a sigh. "The Brotherhood's numbers have been steadily thinning for the past several years, which means there were less and less progeny to be inducted. To replenish our numbers quicker The Hand started recruiting outlaws and mercenaries." The Hand were a group of Brotherhood members who acted as delegators of contracts and enforcers of the Brotherhood's authority, answering only to the Elders.

"Mercenaries?" This bit of news surprised Animal. He was no expert on the Brotherhood, but he knew more than most based on what Kahllah had taught him about the order, but the one thing he knew for certain was, they were selective about membership. "And the Elders are allowing this?"

"The Elders are getting on in years, most of them are too old to be active in the day to day affairs. For the most part they stay tucked away in the mountains, hording money and playing political games. When father was alive he was able to help maintain the balance, but when he died, so did his sway with the Elders," Kahllah said sadly.

This came as somewhat of a shock to Animal. "I didn't realize the old man held so much sway."

"There is much you don't know about our father. Priest was more than some attack dog for the Clarks. He was a man of great respect and influence," Kahllah said proudly.

Priest was a reputed assassin and high-ranking member of the Brotherhood of Blood, but he was also Kahllah and Animal's father. Both were bound to him by blood, but only one of them by genes, though you couldn't tell which was which from their vastly different upbringings. Animal was Priest's biological son, while Kahllah had been adopted. Priest had rescued Kahllah from a cruel man in Africa, who had been keeping her as a slave, and raised the orphan as his own child and apprentice. Kahllah was given the best education and trained by the best killers, to be molded in her adopted father's image. There would be no such luxuries afforded Animal. Priest had left him and his mother when Animal was still very young, so he had no real memories of him except for the hate he harbored for the man who had abandoned him. Animal's childhood was cruel to the point of being inhumane, and he carried the scars of his abuse into adulthood. He had always pledged that if he ever met his biological father, he would kill him. Years later he would have the chance for his reckoning, but things played out far differently than he had expected.

A death sentence had been passed on Animal by a crime lord named Shai Clark, for crimes against his organization. In a strange turn of events, it had been Priest who was sent to carry out the sentence. Instead of killing him, as he had been ordered, Priest defied his boss and spared his son. During their brief time together, Animal learned the truth about his family history and the real reason Priest had left them. Priest had many enemies and couldn't stand the thought of one of them using his family to hurt him, so he distanced himself from Animal and his mother, watching from a distance and secretly manipulating the hands of fate in Animal's life. It didn't exonerate Priest from abandoning Animal, but it gave his son a better understanding of what kind of man he was, and more importantly, closure. In the end, Priest had made the ultimate sacrifice a father could for his son and gave his own life so that Animal would have a second chance at living his. To say that Animal had ever come to love his father would've been a lie, but he had grown to respect him and what he represented, a man willing to make impossible choices for those he loved.

"So, who is running things now?" Animal asked.

"The Hand," Kahllah said in disgust. "Khan claims to speak for the Elders now and anyone who contests him either turns up missing or found guilty of some phantom crime against the Brotherhood."

Animal had heard the name Khan before, but he didn't know much about him except that he was a part of the Hand. "But you're part of the Hand too. Don't you have a say in what goes on?"

"Yes, I am a member of the Hand, but I am still a female . . . the first to ever be given the honor, but it's more in name than anything else. I don't sit very high on the food chain in the eyes of the rest of the Hand."

"Bullshit, Kahllah. I've seen you in action, and you're one of, if not *the* best, at what you do. You earned your position!" Animal insisted.

"I appreciate your confidence in me, little brother, but that isn't how our world works. For as many strides as the Brotherhood has made over the years, it is still a very sexist order. I have a higher kill rate than any active member of the Brotherhood, except for Legion, but my induction into the Hand wasn't due to my success rate, but father's insistence. I am what you would call a *token*," Kahllah said in disgust. "I could break every record, held by every member, and my gender would still limit my authority," she explained.

"Sounds like a load of bullshit to me," Ashanti spoke up. "Maybe it's time for some new leadership in the Brotherhood."

"You aren't the only one who feels that way, Ashanti, and maybe pretty soon we will see the balance of power shift," Kahllah cast her eyes at Animal when she said this. "But enough about murder and politics. We've got places to be."

"Speaking of that, do either of you plan on filling me in on what this job is all about?" Animal asked.

"I'll explain to you on the way. We've got a schedule to keep," Kahllah said and started back across the sand, with Ashanti behind her.

As Animal made to follow them, his cell phone went off. He looked at the caller I.D. and saw that it was Gucci. She hadn't been happy when he left the house. Animal understood why, but he didn't feel like hearing it at that moment. He had to keep his head in the game. With a sigh, he hit the ignore button and dropped the phone back in his pocket before catching up with Kahllah and Ashanti.

# TWO

GUCCI SAT MOTIONLESS; WORDS pursed on her lips but no air in her lungs to push them out. T.J. sat on the floor a few feet away, happily playing with his toys. He waddled over to offer one to their guest, but the little girl simply glared at him as if she wanted to kill him. Gucci had seen that look a million times, but it was unnerving to see it on the face of a child.

Across from Gucci sat her uninvited guest, the one person who could turn her dream into a nightmare – her husband's mistress, Red Sonja. Seeing her in person for the first time, Gucci could almost understand why Animal had fallen for her. She was a pretty Puerto Rican girl, with flawless skin, steel grey eyes and hair the color of a burning forest. She sat in the middle of the living room, Gucci's living room, staring at her as if she was the stranger who had intruded. Gucci had a good mind to pop her in the chin, but she had to maintain her composure in front of the children. Knowing Animal had been with another woman while they were apart hurt her, but when she found out that they'd conceived a child together, it devastated her. She couldn't even look at Celeste because every time she did she saw Animal, and it made her want to vomit. They were almost twins, except she was lighter.

Gucci wondered for the millionth time since Red Sonja had shown up if Animal had known about the child all along and kept it from her. She would've liked to have thought better of him, but she knew first hand that her husband was a man of many secrets, and she could put nothing past him.

"How?" was all Gucci could manage to ask when she finally found her voice.

Sonja cocked her head as if she didn't understand the question. "Animal and I fucked, sometimes with condoms and sometimes without. One of those without times produced Celeste. That's how babies are made. Damn, don't they teach you hood rats anything in public school?"

Gucci felt her anger rising, but remained calm. "If you insist upon insulting me, I'm going to have to ask you to leave my house."

"I'm going to leave, but not before I've spoken my piece. Unless you think you've got the nuts to make me leave?" Sonja asked in a mocking tone. She watched Gucci open and close her fists and it made her smile. "You thinking about trying me, Gucci? Nah, you couldn't be thinking that because you and I both know how it would play out."

"Sonja, I'm not a fighter but I ain't no punk so don't get it fucked up. You better ask somebody about Gucci *Torres*." Gucci put emphasis on the last name to remind her that she and Animal were now married.

"Oh, I know all about you, Gucci. I heard about the little stripes you got when you popped off to save *our* baby daddy.

It's admirable and I'm glad to see you're not a complete waste of flesh, but make no mistake about the difference in our two pedigrees. You've killed and I'm a killer, big difference. While you were sucking off local drug dealers in project stairwells, I was executing paid hits. Don't test me."

"What do you want, Sonja?" Gucci asked, tiring of her games.

"The same thing you want, what's best for my kid."

"Well if it's money you want —"

"Have you not been paying attention?" Sonja cut her off. "I could buy you twice and it wouldn't put a dent in my bank account. You and Animal are rich, but I'm wealthy. I'm not here for your food stamp card, so stop assuming."

"Then stop playing games and tell me why you're here!" Gucci demanded.

The smirk faded from Sonja's face and she became very serious. "Well, I wanted to have this conversation with Animal, but I guess you'll do for now. I'm calling in a favor that Tayshawn owes."

"Animal doesn't owe you anything. Any ties he had to you were left in Puerto Rico."

"I beg to differ, love. If it weren't for me, Animal would still be living on that compound, and under K-Dawg's thumb. He owes and I'm here to collect, period!"

"If you don't want money then what do you want?"

Sonja smiled. "The same thing everybody else wants from Animal. I want him to kill someone."

# THREE

"I AIN'T KILLING NOBODY," ANIMAL SAID FROM the passenger seat of the Black SUV Kahllah had *appropriated* on her way from the airport.

"So you've said at least half a dozen times since we picked you up," Kahllah said sarcastically from behind the wheel. She whipped the big truck like it was a Honda Civic, moving in and out of evening traffic on the 101 South. They were headed into the city.

"Fuck all that, I'm gonna blast on this pussy and everybody with him," Ashanti spat. "I got no mercy for this coward, or anyone else who would fuck with little kids like that. He ain't fit to live, and I'm gonna see to it that he rests in hell before the night is over," Ashanti declared from the back seat. He was holding a .44 bulldog in his hand, absently thumbing the hammer.

Ashanti was always angry, but that night Animal noticed he seemed slightly more vicious than he remembered, and he was one of the few people who understood why. From what Kahllah had revealed to him, their target man was named Thad Klein. Klein was a high profile criminal attorney, who moonlighted as a flesh peddler and pedophile. When he wasn't fighting top dollar cases in courtrooms across the state of California, he was trolling the internet for naïve children to have his way with or to connect with the members of the sick circles he serviced. His specialty was targeting the children of the clients he represented. Klein's latest victim had been the daughter of one of his clients, Caesar "Gordo" Marquez. Gordo was a narcotics trafficker who had recently been sentenced to fifteen years in state prison, thanks in part to Klein intentionally sacking his case. Klein had been trying to lure Gordo's fifteen-year-old daughter away for months, but he couldn't officially put her on the market until he got Gordo out of the way, so he sought to bury him in the deepest, darkest hole he could find. He had it all planned out, but in all his scheming he didn't encounter Gordo being a friend to the Brotherhood.

Klein's crimes hit close to home for Ashanti, because he too had been a victim of abuse. When he was just a snot-nosed kid, Ashanti and his sister, Angela, had been handed over to some men by their mother, Annie, as collateral for a debt she owed them. When Annie couldn't pay, the men sold her children. Ashanti was able to escape and made it back to the hood, but Angela was never seen or heard from again. Animal and Ashanti never spoke in detail about the things that happened to him while he was a captive, but Animal knew they weren't pleasant. One day, maybe his friend would be ready to open up about it and Animal would be there for him when that day came. Ashanti was an adult now, but to Animal he was still his little brother.

They exited the freeway at North Highland Avenue and took it to Hollywood Boulevard. For as long as Animal had been living in California, he could count on one hand how many times he'd ever ventured far into any of the neighboring cities. He went into L.A. whenever he needed to or if Gucci wanted to go shopping, but those trips were rare. California was so culturally different from where he was from that it never felt like home. For as close as Los Angeles was to New York, Animal always felt like an outsider; when Kahllah drove them into West Hollywood he felt especially out of bounds.

Animal could hear Ashanti behind him shuffling uncomfortably when they crossed into the section of the city called Boy's Town. Boy's Town was the hub of Hollywood's gay community, and it was obvious from the time you crossed into it. Rainbow flags hung proudly from shops and windows. Same-sex couples sat at tables, holding hands and chatting over meals or coffee, enjoying the night breeze, while men dressed in outrageous outfits walked the streets, peddling their wares or trying to coax people into one of the bars that lined the streets. To outsiders it would've looked like a circus, but to those who frequented Boy's Town, it was just another Friday night.

"Disgusting," Ashanti said under his breath, as a muscular man wearing a pair of booty shorts waved at him from the doorway of a bar.

Kahllah spared a glance over her shoulder. "I never took you for a homophobe, Ashanti."

"A what?" he didn't understand the phrase.

"She means someone who is uncomfortable around gays," Animal explained.

23

"I ain't uncomfortable around them, I just don't like them," Ashanti said. "When I was growing up, boys liked girls and vice versa. Now it's like these chicks be on dick one day and pussy the next. To me that shit is like trying to play X-box with a PlayStation joystick. It's not a natural fit. Look, if God meant for men to be with men he wouldn't have given the pussies to women. Personally, I blame rap music for all this."

"And what does rap music have to do with it?" Kahllah asked.

"Because these days the rappers dress more like bitches than the bitches, and because they on T.V. people think it's trendy. These niggas are gender confused. Bet you wouldn't ever see Rakim on stage in no fucking dress!" Ashanti laughed.

"I swear you are the most ignorant little son of a bitch I've ever met," Kahllah told him.

"That's because you've never met Cain. Now that's one ignorant muthafucka," Ashanti joked. "So what you think, big homie?" he asked Animal.

"What do I think about what?" Animal had only been half listening to the exchange.

"About all this gay shit," Ashanti motioned around him. "How do you feel about it?"

"I don't feel anything about it, because I'm not a homosexual. That's like you asking me about hockey, I've never played it nor am I a fan of the sport so I don't have an opinion about it," Animal explained.

Ashanti shook his head. "Still the coldest nigga to shit between a pair of shoes. Nothing moves you. Anyhow, Kahllah, what the fuck we doing down here? I thought we was gonna go whack Klein? His office is in downtown L.A."

"I know where he works, but I'm going to catch him where he plays," Kahllah said, pulling over at the curb where a group of women were standing.

The women tensed when they saw the SUV. They were obviously *working* girls. Kahllah rolled the window down and made eye contact with one of them, a tall blonde with tanned skin and big breasts. The blonde excused herself from her girls and approached the car. Ashanti openly ogled the white girl. The red dress she wore hugged her like a second skin and left very little to the imagination. He watched as she slunk around the car to Kahllah's side, leaning in to whisper to her, giving him a full view of her cleavage. Ashanti's mind immediately dipped into the gutter. He didn't mess with prostitutes, but the white girl did give him food for thought.

Kahllah and the blonde spoke in hushed tones. Every few seconds the prostitute would look around cautiously, as if she was expecting someone to jump out behind her. After a few minutes of conversation, Kahllah thanked the blonde and handed her an envelope which Ashanti assumed contained cash. The blonde waved goodbye to Kahllah and was hustling back around the car to the curb, when Ashanti decided to try his luck.

"Yo, ma, how much you charging for that?" Ashanti called after her.

She leaned against the car and looked in the window, sizing Ashanti up. She looked at Kahllah, looking for a sign from her as to how to respond. Kahllah simply shrugged her shoulders. The blonde smiled, showing off two rows of perfect white teeth. When she spoke, her voice was so deep that it almost startled Ashanti. "I'm flattered, baby, but I don't sell fish. I sell sausage," she hiked her dress up, giving him a glimpse of her tucked penis.

Kahllah and the prostitute both busted out laughing. Even Animal couldn't hold his chuckle. Ashanti, however, didn't find it funny. His eyes flashed embarrassment then pure anger.

"You freakish muthafucka!" Ashanti spat out the window, narrowly missing the blonde.

"Fuck you, little thirsty nigga! You're just mad that my dick is probably bigger than yours," the prostitute shot back.

"I got a dick for you, bitch," Ashanti picked up his gun and grabbed the door handle. The prostitute made hurried steps back to the curb. Ashanti would've surely gotten out of the car and shot her had it not been for Kahllah hitting the child locks and trapping him. Even as they pulled off, Ashanti could still be heard screaming obscenities from the back of the car.

# FOUR

"I'M GLAD Y'ALL THOUGHT THAT SHIT WAS funny," Ashanti fumed from the backseat.

"You set yourself up for that one," Animal told him, wiping the tears from the corners of his eyes. Every time he thought about the incident he was overcome with another wave of laughter.

"I should've popped on that nigga-bitch. That shit is entrapment," Ashanti said.

"No, it's *thirst*," Kahllah corrected him. "It serves you right. You got a good chick at home and are out here chasing random women. How do you think it would make Fatima feel if she knew you were out here trying to pay for pussy?"

Ashanti immediately felt like shit. What Kahllah was saying was true, Fatima was a good chick and he loved her with everything he had, but Ashanti was still a man and susceptible to certain urges. He started to argue the point with Kahllah, but decided against it.

Kahllah drove down a few blocks, in the direction that the

prostitute had pointed. She slowed as they passed a tattoo parlor at the end of the strip. The parlor was closed, but there was a light on in one of the apartments on top of it. Kahllah drove for another half block before making a U-turn and parking the SUV.

"The tattoo parlor is a front. Klein owns it, and the apartment above it. It's where he conducts his extracurricular business. Ricky says he's having one of his *showcases* tonight," Kahllah revealed what the prostitute had told her. A showcase was when Klein invited a few of his other clients to his apartment for a private showing of his latest acquisitions.

Animal looked up at the window, trying to get an idea of how many people might be inside the apartment, but a thick curtain covered the window. Something about it didn't feel right. "Kahllah, this shit feels funny. It's eighty something degrees out here, but they've got the windows closed and the curtains drawn. I don't see any air conditioners and the fact that the curtains aren't moving means there's probably not even a fan blowing. You expect me to believe that there are people in there doing anything, other than burning up from the heat? You sure you can trust Ricky?"

Kahllah thought on it. "I've known Ricky a long time, and he's never given me bad information. If he says Klein is in there, he's in there."

Animal saw the uncertainty in here eyes, but didn't question her. This was Kahllah and Ashanti's mission, he was just tagging along.

"The longer we sit here talking shit, the more of God's good air this bastard is taking up. Let's go push these nigga's shits back." He was about to get out of the car when Animal's voice stopped him.

"Kick back for a second, Blood," Animal said, surveying the block. It took him a few seconds to spot what he was looking for. "In all my years of moving around the streets, I've never known a man dealing in Klein's kind of business not to have some sort of security in place," he pointed to the darkened doorway of the tattoo parlor.

None of them had noticed on the first pass, but there was a man dressed in all black pressed against the archway of the entrance to the tattoo parlor. Dangling at his side was a pistol.

"Shit, I didn't even see him," Ashanti admitted.

"Exactly, because you're always looking before you leap," Kahllah scolded. "Klein is going to die tonight, but we're just going to have to be creative about it," Kahllah told him and slid out of the car. She walked to the back of the SUV, popped the hatch and retrieved one of two duffel bags she kept back there. "Get in the passenger's seat," she told Ashanti. "Animal, take the wheel."

Animal wasn't sure what was going on, but he knew better than to question it because Kahllah would probably just give him another generic answer, so he would just observe for the moment. Ashanti got into the passenger seat, while Kahllah took his place in the back and Animal took the wheel. To Animal and Ashanti's surprise, Kahllah began undressing in the backseat.

"Eyes front, Ashanti," Kahllah said as if she could feel him trying to watch her through the rearview mirror.

"I was just trying to make sure I could see if anyone was coming up behind us," Ashanti smirked. He turned to Animal. "She always think I'm on some bullshit."

"Most of the time you are," Animal shot back good-naturedly.

"Okay, you guys are good," Kahllah said after a few minutes. Animal was surprised by what he saw, but Ashanti just smirked.

Kahllah had changed into a black catsuit, with a thin custom-made bulletproof vest. It was no thicker than a golf sweater, but lined with steel plates covering all her vital organs. Strapped across her back were two blades that looked like oversized meat cleavers. A black cowl covered her head and neck, leaving only her face visible. Even with her painted lips and seductive eyes, Kahllah still looked quite menacing.

"Don't stare at me like that, it's making me uncomfortable," Kahllah told Animal.

"My bad, but this is my first time ever seeing the Black Lotus," he smirked. Animal had heard about Kahllah's Black Lotus persona, but had never seen her first-hand and he was impressed.

"Consider yourself fortunate. Usually the first time a man lays eyes on the Black Lotus is the last time he ever lays eyes on anything," Kahllah said. She meant it as a joke, but the humor was lost in the serious edge to her tone. "Ashanti, I'm going to take care of our friend in front then I want you to go around the back and cover the rear door in case someone tries to bolt. There will be no mercy for this pervert or his ilk. Anyone who comes out of that door, who isn't me, dies."

"Now you're speaking my language," Ashanti said happily. He didn't care who he got to kill, as long as he got to kill someone. He had been waiting all night to collect his pint of blood and his moment was almost at hand.

"And what do you need me to do?" Animal asked.

Kahllah took her time, sliding a mask down over her face.

It was made of steel that had been blackened so deep that it no longer cast even the faintest reflection of light. In the forehead was carved a black lotus flower. "Keep the engine running and stay out of the way. If I need you, which I doubt, I'll contact you with this," she tossed Animal a small hand radio.

Animal had only taken his eyes off Kahllah long enough to catch the radio, but it was enough time for her to vanish from the vehicle. Animal had never even heard the door open.

"Don't worry, you'll get used to her doing that," Ashanti said, picking up on his slack-jawed look. "Kahllah has a knack for moving without being seen."

"So it would seem," Animal agreed. "What strange twist of fate threw y'all two together?"

Ashanti shrugged. "I can't pinpoint one specific time or another. It's like after everything we went through with Shai brought us together and being there for you while you were locked up kept us together. Me and Kahllah got real close while you were away."

Animal raised an eyebrow. "How close?"

"Not like that," Ashanti laughed. "Kahllah is like a big sister to me. She's been teaching me a lot bout the business."

"So, you're making your bones as a paid assassin now?" Animal asked.

"I'm making my bones as anything that will keep me and mine from starving," Ashanti shot back. "I mostly ride out with Kahllah for shits and giggles, but it's had its benefits beyond the extra cash. I'm carving out my legacy."

"How do you figure?" Animal asked curiously.

"Dig, I ain't saying I'm ready to join the Brotherhood or nothing like that, but for a few minutes of work I sometimes make more than I can standing around on the block. I've been putting in work in the streets for years. I got more hood stripes than any two niggas running a crew, but to everybody I'm still *little Ashanti*. Kahllah said it's because I still carry myself like a common hoodlum, and she's trying to help me be more than that. She's been teaching me things, like discipline and how to talk to people so I can navigate amongst these circles and not seem out of place. She calls it blending. The fact that I get to blow nigga's heads off for money is just a bonus," he laughed.

"Murder is a dirty business, Ashanti."

"Indeed it is," Ashanti agreed, "but there's no denying that I'm good at it. I should be, since I've been around it all my life. I know I don't have to tell you all this, because it was you who showed me my first dead body, remember?"

Animal indeed remembered . . . he remembered it well, because it was the night his life would be forever changed.

It was the night Animal would have his final reckoning with a man named Eddie. Eddie was Animal's mother's boyfriend, and also the man who killed her. Eddie had tormented Animal for most of his life, and treated his mother like shit, but the drugs kept her with him. Years after Animal had already run away, Eddie and his mother finally broke up, but it was Eddie who ended things, in a very fatal way. He had given Animal's mother H.I.V and she died a slow and painful death. Animal had always vowed to murder Eddie, and thanks to Ashanti, he would have his chance.

Eddie had been laying low since the death of Animal's mother, but Ashanti had the good fortune of spotting him up in Connecticut. It had been in the same neighborhood where

Ashanti's child kidnappers had kept him. With Ashanti leading the way, Animal and Tech went to pay a call on Eddie.

They rushed the house, subduing the woman who was renting it and her brother, while Animal trapped Eddie in one of the bedrooms. He knew from the insane look in Animal's eyes that he was surely a dead man, so like the coward he was, he sought something to use in the form of leverage . . . a little girl who had been sleeping in the princess bed a few feet away.

"You take one more step, and I'll cut her," Eddie threatened. He had a kitchen knife pressed against her throat.

"You're a killer and a coward, Eddie," Animal spat.

"Yeah, and I'm also a survivor," Eddie said. "Now back the fuck up or I'm gonna split this little bitch open."

"This is between me and you, Eddie. Let that child go and take your medicine like a man," Animal challenged. He wanted to tear Eddie up bad as hell, but didn't want to risk hitting the little girl.

Eddie laughed. "Nigga, you done seen one movie too many. Ain't no happy endings in the ghetto and ain't no honor among thieves. What's gonna happen next is, you're gonna put that gun down and me and this kid are gonna walk out of here, unharmed."

"And what makes you think I won't just smoke you and her?" Animal asked.

"Because I know you," Eddie said matter-of-factly. "I hear you're making a name for yourself in the streets, but that heart of yours is still tender. For as bad as you wanna kill me, you're more worried about hitting this kid by accident. Now drop that burner, so I can be on my way, and, if I have to ask you again, I might slip and cut her throat by accident."

Animal hesitated for a moment, before finally dropping his gun. He was furious not only because he would miss his chance to kill Eddie, but also because years later, Eddie was still able to play on his insecurities and come out on top.

"You know I'm going to hunt you to the ends of the earth, right? Even if I don't get you tonight, I'll get you eventually," he promised.

"I believe you'll give it your best shot, but, as you can see, Ol' Eddie ain't so easy to kill. Now if you'll excuse me—"

Eddie's body went stiff. He released the little girl and began clawing at his back. When he turned, Animal saw two things— a pair of scissors sticking out of Eddie's back, and Ashanti. During the standoff, he'd snuck around to the side of the house and climbed in through the first floor window of the child's room and got the drop on Eddie. He was the only one of the three who entered the house that didn't have a gun, but he'd snatched a pair of scissors from the living room, thinking they might come in handy, and they did.

Seizing the moment, Animal scooped the Pretty Bitch off the ground and let it rock. The first bullet hit Eddie high in the chest and bounced him off the wall. Animal hit him again and again, causing Eddie's body to do a little dance before falling to the ground. Eddie was down, but still breathing.

Animal walked over to Eddie and stood over him. His eyes were rolling around in his head, trying to find something to focus on.

"Look at me," Animal ordered. Eddie's eyes instinctively went to the voice. "On behalf of my mother and every other person whose life you've ever ruined, I cast you back to the pit of hell that you crawled out of." He fired two shots into Eddie's face, ending his existence. "May God show no mercy on your soul." Animal shot him once more for good measure.

Ashanti was standing there in a numb state, staring at Eddie's dead body. Blood dripped from the hand he had been holding the scissors in when he stabbed him. Ashanti had never seen a dead body before, and couldn't seem to tear his eyes away.

Animal looked at the little boy, studying him. Ashanti wouldn't meet his gaze. Animal tilted Ashanti's chin so that he had no choice but to look him in the eyes. "Blood on my hands . . . blood on yours. Do you understand?"

Ashanti was too stunned to speak, so he just nodded. He couldn't articulate it at the time, but he knew that Animal was letting him know that if he ever thought about telling the story of what had happened that his hands were just as dirty as Animal's. He didn't have to worry about Ashanti telling. Even at that early age he understood the code of the streets, and was already experienced at living by them. He not only understood why Animal had done what he'd done, but he respected it. It was that night that the bond was formed between the two of them, a bond forged by tragedy and sealed by blood.

"To this day, I've never spoken to another living soul about that night, not even Tech after it happened," Ashanti told him.

"Because you're a good soldier, and always have been. You were the one person I've always been able to depend on," Animal told him. "That was a bad night," Animal added.

An uncomfortable silence hung between them. Ashanti looked at Animal as if he wanted to say something, but couldn't find the words. Something was on his heart.

"Don't think about it, just say it," Animal told him, picking up on his tabulation.

"It ain't bout nothing, I'm just glad to see you free . . . like *for real* free, no more bullshit," Ashanti said.

"I'm happy to be free, but I wouldn't say that my new freedom isn't without some of the same bullshit. If that was the case then I probably wouldn't be sitting in the car with you two fools," Animal joked.

"You know old habits die hard," Ashanti said with a smile. His face suddenly became serious. "Look big homie, I just wanted to tell you that I'm sorry I didn't get up to visit you like that when you were locked down. I meant to come, but I just had a lot of shit going on, ya know?"

"Yeah, I can dig that, little brother, and I totally understand. When you're inside, it's like time stops when you fall into that prison routine. Out in the world, things keep moving. We soldiers, Ashanti, and as soldiers we understand that prison comes with the territory. I ain't saying it like going to prison is a badge of honor or no shit like that, but when you're in the streets it strengthens your chances of going. When that time comes, you buckle down, do your time. Getting caught up in what's going on in the world only makes it harder."

"Is that what you did to get through your time, forget about everybody?" Ashanti asked.

Animal laughed. He hadn't meant it to mock Ashanti, but the genuine curiosity in his question took him back to a time when Ashanti was still a little boy, picking Animal's brain for information. "Man, I only had eighteen months, not eighteen years," Animal said. "Granted, even one day in prison is one day too many, but my bid wasn't the worst. Of course I missed my son and my lady, but because I was so close to the city, Gucci was able to come visit me on the regular, before she moved out here to set things up for us. Outside of that, I did a lot of reading and working out to help me pass the time."

"I hear the homies are strong in the prison system," Ashanti said.

"Please believe it, we definitely had numbers up in there but I didn't get into all that gang shit while I was locked up. It wasn't conducive to who I was striving to become. All that kind of shit does is bring problems that I didn't want."

"So you saying you ain't bout that *five* no more?" Ashanti asked.

"I'm always gonna be about that because it's a part of who I am, but if you mean taking life over colors, no I ain't bout that. I think it stopped being about that for me when I killed Eddie. When I was young, coming up under Tango and Gladiator, all I wanted to do was prove that I was the hardest Blood out, but after a while it was no longer about colors, it was about having a purpose. In my entire life, killing had been the only thing I was ever good at. For the first time people needed me, instead of the other way around. Killing got good to me. I had been the prey for so long that it felt good to be the predator. Every time I dropped a nigga, I didn't see their faces, but the faces of someone who had done me wrong in life. Death became my drug of choice and I was a stone cold junkie."

"I remember those days," Ashanti said, thinking back to how things used to be. Animal could kill a man in the most gruesome ways and never bat an eye. He was cold, calculated and Ashanti wanted to be just like him. "What changed?" It was a question Ashanti felt like he already knew the answer to, but he had never asked it out loud.

"Gucci changed all that," Animal said honestly. "Before I met her I was just out there throwing caution to the wind, and doing whatever to whomever. I didn't care about the repercussions, having somebody in my life who could potentially get hurt because of my bullshit made me slow down and really start to think about the things I was out there doing. I changed for her."

"So you saying the killer is dead?" Ashanti asked.

"Nah, the killer in me is alive and well, I'm just better at establishing who is in control," Animal said.

"See, that's what I'm getting at, Animal. Kahllah says I need to learn control, but it ain't as easy as she thinks when you come from what we come from. These niggas I deal with day in and day out are savages and they only respect other savages. I ain't good at diplomacy. If you out here foul and your name gets pulled out the hat then its lights out, Blood. Straight like that."

"I feel you, Ashanti, but what's the end game?" Animal asked.

Ashanti cocked his head to one side. "I don't follow you."

"I mean, to what end are you playing the game? When it's all said and done, what are you in it for?"

Ashanti looked at Animal, weighing the question. "To die rich and notorious," he said seriously.

His answer saddened Animal. Chronologically Ashanti was an adult, but mentally he was still a young man wandering the dark path . . . the path Animal had set him on, just as Gladiator had done for him years prior.

38

Before their conversation could go any further, something bounced across the hood of the car, startling both of them. They weren't sure what it was, but it had left a bloodstain on the windshield.

Chester had been on his feet all day, and half the night, with no signs that he'd be able to relax anytime soon. Normally, doing security for Thad Klein was a cakewalk, and largely consisted of him spending his days watching Netflix on his phone or driving Klein back and forth, but not that day. Klein had kept Chester running around checking on this or that, and double-checking security. With all the cocaine Klein did, he was always paranoid, but that day he was more so.

A sound coming from the small cove on the side of the tattoo parlor, where the dumpster was kept, caught Chester's attention. It sounded like a wounded animal. Chester started to ignore it until he remembered how Klein felt about his cats. He treated those animals better than he did people. One time, one of Mr. Klein's prized Persian cats had gotten out of the apartment and got hit by a car. He went ballistic and fired the guy who was doing security on the apartment that day, calling him negligent. Chester needed his job, so he reasoned it was better to be safe than sorry.

Chester crept around the side of the building to the dumpster with is gun hanging at his side. It was dark around the cove of the dumpster, so he fished a small flashlight from his pocket and flicked it on. At first he didn't see anything but trash, but on his second sweep he caught it. One of Mr. Klein's cats had gotten out, and it was lying on the ground, meowing sorrowfully. Chester could see the cat's legs twitching, but it made no attempt to get up. Chester figured the cat must've fallen from the window of the upstairs apartment and hurt itself.

"So much for cats always landing on their feet," Chester chuckled. He knelt down to check the extent of the cat's injuries. For the most part, the cat seemed to be intact, except for the bone protruding from its neck. It was a clean break, so it couldn't have been caused by a fall. By the time two and two made four in Chester's mind, it was already too late.

Chester spun, with his gun raised, at the same time Kahllah's blade cut through is wrist, severing the hand holding the gun. The scream that he was trying to muster died in his throat, when the second blade slit it. The last thing he saw before the light faded from his eyes was the black mask staring down at him.

After making sure Chester was dead, Kahllah waved her hands at the SUV to give Ashanti the signal, but he didn't notice. He and Animal were so deep into whatever they were talking about that neither of them saw Kahllah giving the signal. "Fucking amateurs," Kahllah cursed under her breath. She needed a way to get their attention without tipping Klein off, and looking down at Chester's dead body she had just the solution.

Animal and Ashanti got out of the car at the same time, guns dawn, and keeping one eye on the street. When they reached the front of the car, they found a human head lying just under the front bumper.

"What the fuck?" Animal frowned.

"It's Kahllah's signal," Ashanti said. He looked across the

street just in time to see her slip inside the tattoo parlor. "Game time," he told Animal and jogged across the street.

Animal was about to take off after him, when he remembered his roll in the caper. "No wet work," he mumbled to himself. All Animal could do was lean against the truck, brooding, while Ashanti made his way around the back of the building and into the action.

# FIVE

KAHLLAH SLITHERED THROUGH THE DARKENED TATTOO PARLOR like a shadow. Through the front window she could see Ashanti flash across en route to take up his position in the back. For all Ashanti's character flaws, he was a sharp and willing apprentice.

At the back of the parlor there was a door that led to the apartment upstairs. It was an older model door, with a small window at the top of it. Kahllah removed what looked like a car antenna with a dental mirror on the end from her vest, and extended it. She slowly raised the mirror so that she could see what or who was behind the door. It was a narrow stairwell, barely big enough to fit more than one person at a time. In such close quarters, her cleavers would be useless, as there wasn't enough room to swing them effectively. At the top of the stairs was a man, sitting in a chair reading a magazine. She didn't see a gun, but she knew he had one. The way the chair was turned, he would be able to see anyone who came through the door and get the drop on them if necessary. She was at a disadvantage, but it wasn't the first time and surely wouldn't be the last. Her attack had to be swift and precise.

Kahllah used one hand to yank the door open, while letting the other slide to her thigh, where she kept a dagger strapped. The man at the top of the stairs noticed her just as she flung the blade. The dagger whistled end over end and found a comfortable spot in the man's throat. Kahllah's feet moved swiftly, yet silently up the stairs, catching the man's body before it could fall and laying it gently on the stairs. After retrieving her dagger from his throat, she moved to the apartment door.

She placed her ear to the door and listened for a few moments. She could hear the sounds of music playing softly, but no voices, which she found unusual. If Klein was showcasing children to clients, she expected to hear at least some type of chatter. Using the tip of her dagger, she quickly picked the lock and slipped inside the apartment. The living room was dimly lit, with just a few lamps turned on here and there. In the middle of the floor there was a pile of hastily discarded clothes, those of a grown man's and a child's. Kahllah's heart raced, fearful that she had arrived too late to stop Klein from whatever he had planned for his child hostage.

She could hear the sounds of voices coming from one of the back bedrooms. The first was that of a man, the second of a child presumably whimpering. Kahllah crept across the slick linoleum floor of the hallway, towards the bedroom where she heard the voices. She took her time, checking each room as she passed, making sure there were no surprises laying in wait for her. As she got closer, they became louder. There was definitely a child in danger. Drawing both her cleavers, Kahllah kicked the bedroom door open and rushed inside. She had expected to see some horrific scene of a child being violated, but there wasn't a child in sight.

Sitting on the other side of the room, in a chair near the window, was her mark, Thad Klein. Klein was dressed as usual in an immaculately tailored suit, with his dark hair perfectly combed. His manicured hands were folded over his knee. Playing on the television in front of him was a fetish pornography DVD. That's where the voices had been coming from.

Klein didn't even bother to turn his head to acknowledge her presence. He raised his hand for silence, and stared intently at the television. The actors on the screen were nearing the climax of the scene. Klein watched as if in a trance; the sight of him and what was playing on the screen disgusted Kahllah. With a swing of one of her cleavers, Kahllah severed the cord and the screen went black.

Klein looked disappointed. "And it was just about to get to the good part," he shook his head. "No worries, I've seen that particular film over a dozen times and I know how it ends."

"Speaking of ends, yours is at hand, pedophile," Kahllah told him. The filters in her mask distorted her voice and made it sound almost mechanical.

Klein slowly rose to his feet, regarding her. "Not quite what I expected, considering your reputation," Klein said in an easy tone. "I don't supposed I could offer to double whatever price has been put on my head to get you to turn around and act like we've never seen each other, could I?"

"No amount of money could make me turn a blind eye to your evil, Klein. You are the devil and as is the will of my Lord, I will send you back to hell for what you've done to those children." Kahllah told him.

"I had a feeling you would say as much, so how about we go with offer number two," Klein said with a sinister edge to his voice. "I fill you full of holes and go down in history as the guy who took out the *Black Lotus*."

When Klein had called her by name, an alarm had gone off in Kahllah's head. She was about to move on Klein when she noticed several red dots magically appear all over her body. She cut her eyes to the doorway, already knowing what she would see. There were several armed men with automatic weapons trained on her. She'd checked the rooms and didn't see anyone, so they had to have come into the apartment after she did. They were expecting her. It was a trap and Kahllah had walked right into it.

Standing around and doing nothing was driving Animal insane. He was used to being in the thick of things and riding the pine wasn't sitting well with him. Every few seconds he found himself looking up at the window, wondering how things were going with Kahllah and her kill. He wanted to be involved in the bloodshed so bad that he could literally taste it, but he had promised Gucci. It was bad enough that he had rode out with Kahllah and Ashanti, but spilling blood would only make things worse. He would do his part as the lookout and collect his money, but he didn't like it. Animal sat on the hood of the truck and fired up a cigarette. From his elevated vantage point, he could see down the entire strip. On the next block he saw the transgender prostitute Ricky and his crew, trying to flag down tricks. A van pulled up at the curb and Ricky approached the passenger's side window. He could see Ricky saying something to someone in the car and pointing in the direction of the building he had sent Kahllah into. Suddenly, Animal got an eerie feeling in the pit of his gut. The van pulled away from the curb and sped down the street. It screeched to a halt in front of the tattoo parlor, and several armed men spilled out and rushed inside. They had been set up.

Animal knew that Ashanti was in the back, so he was probably oblivious as to what was going on. He was about to grab the radio Kahllah had given him to warn her when he heard the gunshot. He didn't have time to think, so he grabbed the leather holster, holding his Pretty Bitches, from the backseat and reacted. "Forgive me, Gucci," Animal whispered, before drawing his guns and charging the tattoo parlor.

Over all her years of service to the Brotherhood, Kahllah had an almost flawless track record. Even in her Initiate years of training, she had always been at the top of her class. She had been raised for the sole purpose of taking lives, so she had an edge over the other Initiates, who had to be taught to embrace death. She had no children, no family and no ties to anything in the outside world. Her ability to detach herself from all emotions and focus on nothing but the job was what made her such an efficient killer. That night she allowed her focus to slip and found herself on the wrong end of a death threat.

"You can drop the blades," Klein ordered her. When she looked like she was thinking about making a move, Klein nodded to one of his men. The man shot the ground near Kahllah's foot. "The next one is in your head. Now drop the blades." Kahllah reluctantly threw her blades to the ground. "That's better, now we can talk," he moved closer to get a better look, but was careful not to move too close. Even outnumbered and outgunned, the Black Lotus was still deadly. "Nothing to say for yourself? I hear you like to quote scripture before you kill your victims. What does your good book say about situations like this?" he taunted her.

"When the perishable puts on the imperishable, and the mortal puts on immortality, then shall come to pass the saying that is written: "Death is swallowed up in victory." She quoted Corinthians.

"And what the fuck is that supposed to mean?" Klein asked.

"It means your victory will be a short one, pedophile. Even if I fall here today, another flower will grow in my place. You will be a hunted man for all your days," Kahllah told him.

"Somehow, I doubt that. Everybody who pats you on your back isn't your friend. I think you've overestimated your value, doll," Klein chuckled.

Klein continued to talk, but Kahllah was deaf to everything else he said. It was his previous statement that sent a chill down her spine. He called her *doll*, meaning he knew she was a female. Very few outside of the Brotherhood knew that the Black Lotus was a female. If Klein had that information then her betrayal went far deeper than just Ricky.

"I asked if you had any last words before we made a mess of you?" Klein repeated the question.

"Yes," Kahllah said in an all too calm voice. "So does my lord speak with my voice, he smites with my hands!" Kahllah whipped her hands out and two thin chains shot from her wrists. The steel hooks on the ends of them sank into the flesh of Klein's left arm and his collarbone. Kahllah yanked the chains, snapping Klein to her like he was at the end of a rubber band. Wrapping a length of the chain around his neck, Kahllah kept

Klein's body between her and the shooters like a human shield. "You boys might be good, but I don't think any of you are good enough to take me down without hitting your employer. Now make a path and let me through," she ordered. The men looked hesitant, so she tightened the chain around Klein's neck, causing the hook to tear at the flesh over his collarbone.

"Do what she says!" Klein yelped.

The men stood down, and opened up a space for Kahllah to walk through. One of them looked like he was thinking about playing hero, but Klein's pleading eyes told him to hold his position. She made sure to keep Klein close and her back to the wall. Kahllah slipped past the men and was now in the hallway and headed to the door. She was just passing the kitchen when something smashed into the side of her head. The world swam and for a minute, things went black. When Kahllah was finally able to regain her wits, she was lying on her back with several guns trained on her and Klein was free.

Klein hovered over her, bloodied and angry. "You filthy cunt," he kicked her in the face, knocking Kahllah's mask off. "Get this pretty bitch up," he ordered his men. Two of the gunmen pulled Kahllah to her feet and pinned her to the wall. "First, I was just going to stick to the plan and kill you," Klein undid his belt, "but now I'm going to fuck you first."

When Klein was close enough, Kahllah raised both her legs and jackknifed the heels of her boots into his chest, sending him crashing into the wall behind him. She had been trying to break his ribs to puncture his heart, but because she was being held at an awkward angle, her aim was off, and she only succeeded in knocking the wind out of him. One of the men holding her punched her in the face twice, dazing her and taking enough of the fight out of her for two more men to come over and secure her legs.

When Klein was able to catch his breath, he stalked over to Kahllah, smiling, with his wrinkled pink dick in his hand. "You're a fighter, huh? I like it when they fight. Strip this bitch," he told his men.

When Kahllah saw the look in Klein's eyes, she was transported to her years amongst the slave traders and the things they did to her. She would rather die than have a man force himself on her. Kahllah managed to get one of her arms loose. The man who had been holding her was taken totally by surprise, when she jammed her fingers into his eyes and blinded him. She would've torn his throat out next, had two more men not come to grab her arm. Kahllah struggled against them while they tore away her belts and harnesses, trying to get her body suit off, but there was little she could do. One of them took a knife and cut the lower half of her body suit down the middle, exposing her shaved vagina.

Klein moved close enough to where she could smell the cheap scotch on his breath. Klein kept his eyes locked on Kahllah's while he forced his fingers inside her. He smiled when he saw her eyes twitch, and forced his fingers deeper inside her. Kahllah's eyes welled with tears, but she would not cry. She wouldn't give him the satisfaction. Klein removed his slick fingers from her vagina and smelled them, before slipping his fingers into his mouth and sucking her juices off.

"Sweetest flower I've ever tasted," Klein breathed over her lips.

"And it'll also be the last flower you ever taste," a voice called from the door.

Klein turned and saw a wild haired young man standing in the doorway, holding two very big pistols. His lips parted into a sneer, and Klein could see the faintest hints of diamonds across his teeth. It was a small gesture, but it made Klein's bowels shift. The Black Lotus was a dangerous killer, but the young man who had entered the apartment was death himself.

Klein had just thrown himself to the floor when Animal squeezed the triggers on his guns. Just above him, the heads of the men who had been holding Kahllah's arms, exploded like rotten tomatoes. The remaining gunmen abandoned their duties of restraining the Black Lotus, and drew their weapons. Animal moved like a blur, and ducked under the first wave of shots, sliding on his knees across the linoleum floor, firing one gun at a time. While the gunmen's shots were wild and frantic, Animal's were timed and precise. He laced two more of the gunmen, piercing their heart and small intestines, respectively. Animal skidded to a stop next to one of the men he had seen holding Kahllah's leg. He wasn't quite dead yet, but it was an easy fix. Animal dumped two bullets in his face for good measure.

Klein was scrambling down the hallways towards one of the bedrooms. He was firing a .32 blindly over his shoulder, doing more damage to the ceiling and walls than anything else. Animal had a clear shot at his head, but Kahllah stopped him.

"He's mine!" Kahllah told him and took off after Klein.

Animal wasn't sure what had happened to Kahllah before he'd arrived, but the feral look in her eyes frightened him. Not sure what else to do, he followed her.

Kahllah rounded the corner into the bedroom, and ducked just as a bullet hit the door above her head. She went low, dropping into a roll, she retrieved one of her discarded cleavers, and popped up directly in front of Klein. He raised his gun to get off another shot, but she effortlessly knocked the gun away, and held his arm in a death grip. Kahllah held him, immobile, staring at his fingers as if they were something vile. With a swipe of her cleaver she removed every finger on his hand. Klein screamed in pain with each snip. He struggled to free himself from her grip, but Kahllah had a firm hold on him.

"Worm," she twisted his hand, breaking his wrist, "pedophile," she twisted again, snapping his elbow, "rapist," she dislocated his shoulder. Klein tried to fall to the ground, but she yanked him back to his feet by his useless arm, drawing a whimper from him. "For your crimes against those children, you have been sentenced to die, but for your crimes against me, I condemn you to a lifetime of suffering."

Animal had seen and done some gruesome things in his lifetime, but if you stacked them all together they'd still come up short measured against what Kahllah did to Klein in that bedroom. She retrieved her harnesses from the hallways and came back into the room and knelt beside Klein. From one of the pouches she removed a small butane torch and began superheating the edge of one of the cleavers. She needed the blade to be hot so that Klein's wounds would cauterize and he wouldn't bleed out before she was done with him. Kahllah started with his eyes, bringing them to a boil in his sockets. She took her time with the rest of him, cutting away little pieces here and there, while he wailed and begged for mercy. By the time Kahllah had finished with him, Klein was laying on the ground in pieces like a Mr. Potato Head toy, barely breathing, but still alive and in a great deal of pain.

When Kahllah turned to Animal, she looked like something out of a horror movie. Her face and what were left of her clothes were covered in blood. The cleaver was still clutched firmly in her hand, dripping with blood. Her eyes had retained some of their composure, but the anger still burned brightly. A lone tear ran down her cheek, tracing a line through the sea of crimson.

Animal could feel her pain all the way from where he was standing. He knew what it was like to be violated, and his heart ached for her. "Kahllah – " he began, but she cut him off.

"There is nothing to say," she said just above a whisper. "We will never speak of this . . . ever. Do you understand?"

"Yeah, you got that," Animal agreed. His eyes roamed over to what was left of Klein. He looked like a lab experiment gone wrong, limbless and wriggling around on the floor. A wet gurgling sound emitted from his throat. Whether he was trying to scream or speak, Animal couldn't tell because Kahllah had cut out his tongue. "I should finish him off. It's wrong to leave him here like this," he aimed one of his Pretty Bitches at Klein, ready to put him out of his misery.

"No," Kahllah said sternly. "I want him to live so that he may carry my message to those who have sought to betray me. The Black Lotus is not so easily taken out."

"Well don't you think you should've at least found out from him who it was that set you up before you cut his tongue out?" Animal asked.

"I don't need him to tell me what I fear I already know," Kahllah said sadly. There were only a handful of people who had the resources and intelligence to lay a trap for someone of the Black Lotus's skill, and the list of those who had motive to want her out of the way was even shorter.

Just then the bedroom door swung open, causing Animal and Kahllah both to spin on the defensive. Animal was about to squeeze the triggers on his guns when he realized that it was only Ashanti. He stood in the doorway, gun raised and looking at the carnage in wide-eyed shock. When his eyes landed on Kahllah, covered in blood and with her privates exposed, his look of shock turned into one of concern.

"Big sis, what happened?" Ashanti asked, ready to punish whoever it was who had hurt her.

"Nothing my brother and I couldn't handle," Kahllah patted Ashanti lovingly on the cheek, leaving bloody fingerprints. "I'll meet you back at the truck," she told them and left the apartment.

For the first time Ashanti noticed that Animal was holding his pistols. It was the first time he'd seen Animal holding a gun in years and it filled his heart with great pride. "So much for promises, huh?"

Animal looked down at his guns. He thought that he would've felt ashamed for breaking his promise to Gucci, but instead, he felt alive . . . more alive than he'd felt in years. "I guess so."

"Damn, Blood, how y'all gonna lay everybody down before I got my taste? I came all the way out here to Fag-Town and ain't nothing left for me to do," Ashanti said, sounding like a disappointed kid who had just found out he had to attend summer school and couldn't go away to camp.

Animal suddenly had a fiendish idea. He knelt beside Klein, careful not to get blood on his clothes, began searching his pockets. It took a second, but he eventually found what he was looking for. "Bingo," he smiled.

"What you doing, man?" Ashanti asked.

Animal twirled a key ring on his finger. "About to make this night worth your while."

The minute Ricky had heard the shooting, he got out of dodge. He felt bad about what he had done to Kahllah because she had always been so kind to him. He'd first met her a few years back when she was on the West Coast doing a story on the secret life of Transgender Prostitutes. She didn't treat Ricky like some sideshow freak, as everyone else had done. She was kind, respectful and caring. She'd even helped him find a room to rent because he was living on the streets. Kahllah had been one of the very few bright spots in his life since he had been out on his own, working the streets.

For as foul as what Ricky had done might've seemed, he felt like he didn't have a choice. When he had been approached about helping lay the trap, Ricky was against it, but they made an offer he couldn't refuse. They had taken his parents and young nephew hostage. He was given a choice between helping set Kahllah up or watching while his family was butchered. Ricky's parents hadn't said two words to him since he'd come out of the closet and he couldn't have cared less what happened to them, but his nephew was innocent. Reluctantly, Ricky agreed. Now, because of him, Kahllah was dead.

Ricky wiped the tears from his eyes, careful not to smear his makeup. The night was still young and he had a quota to make, or risk the wrath of his pimp. There was no way he could work the strip anymore that night, so he move a few blocks down to one of the quieter streets. There wasn't as much traffic as the strip, and it was mostly worked by outlaws and drug addicts, but it would have to do, at least for the night. A Mercedes came slow coasting down the streets. It was white with tinted windows, and shining like new money. It didn't take long for the misfits who worked that section of Boy's Town to come crawling out of whatever cracks and crevasses they'd been hiding in. They were a homely looking lot compared to Ricky. They were on him like vultures, but that was only because he hadn't seen Ricky.

The man-whore hiked his skirt a bit so that his ass cheeks were visible, and sashayed across the driver's line of vision. As expected, the driver took one look at her and shooed the others away. When the Benz pulled up in front of Ricky, his walk was triumphant, flipping his long blonde weave and rolling his eyes at the other prostitutes. He had snagged the prize.

The driver rolled the passenger window down. The dome light was out, so Ricky was only able to see flashes of the driver's face in the headlights of the other cars passing them. "What's good? What that mouth do?" He called out to Ricky.

"It'll do whatever you want it to for a hundred bucks, sugar," Ricky said, leaning deep into the open passenger window. In the pale light of a passing truck, he was able to see the driver's face clearly for the first time. It only took Ricky a few seconds to realize where he had seen the driver before, but by then it was already too late.

"Can it swallow a bullet?" Ashanti asked, jamming the bulldog in Ricky's mouth and pulling the trigger twice. Ashanti didn't wait for the body to hit the ground before he pulled off. Animal had kept true to his word and made the night worth Ashanti's while. If he wasn't sure before, he was sure then that his big homie was back on deck.

Rumor had it that a half hour later, when the police finally arrived to find Ricky's body, smoke was still seeping out of his mouth from the bullets Ashanti put in his throat.

"Man that felt good!" Ashanti boasted, once they were back inside the SUV with Kahllah. They'd abandoned Klein's car a few blocks away. "Animal, that was a slick ass idea you had about rolling on that He-she with Klein's car, but what made you want to kill him?"

"Because it was Ricky who set us up. I saw him talking to the guys who ambushed Kahllah," Animal revealed.

"That's some cold shit," Ashanti shook his head in disgust. "Kahllah, I should've bet you some money on all that shit you was talking about being able to trust that freak. You're the main one always talking that 'trust no one but your own shit'," he did his scary voice imitation. "What you got to say for yourself now?"

"Fuck you, Ashanti!" Kahllah snapped.

"Damn, who pissed in your Cheerios? I was only playing. Fuck is your problem?" Ashanti asked.

"Leave it alone, Ashanti," Animal told him. He knew Ashanti didn't mean any harm, but after what Kahllah had gone through, it was no time for jokes. Animal felt his cell phone vibrating in his pocket, and removed it to check the screen. It was the voicemail notification, but he also had fifteen missed calls from Gucci. Something was wrong. He quickly dialed her back and waited while the phone rang. Each time it rang, he felt his heart beat a little faster in his chest. He'd hoped nothing had happened to her or T.J. while he was out committing murders with Kahllah and Ashanti. To his relief, she finally picked up. "What's wrong babe?" he asked, in a concerned tone. Gucci was talking so fast that he almost couldn't understand her. "Wait, slow down. What???" Animal's mouth dropped, as Gucci explained the situation. "Okay, I'll be right there." Animal said and ended the call.

Ashanti looked at his friend and the expression on his face made him uneasy. He wasn't sure what Gucci had said to him on the phone, but whatever it was made him turn white as a ghost. "Everything good?" he asked.

"Nah, everything isn't good. I need to get home, A.S.A.P."

#  SIX

FOR A LONG WHILE ALL ANIMAL COULD do was stare in stunned silence, with his mouth agape. The room felt like it was spinning and his heart was pumping blood to his face and head at such an alarming rate that he felt like he might pass out. He needed to sit down, but didn't trust his legs to carry him the few feet to the closest chair. It felt like a bad dream and no matter how hard he tried, he couldn't wake up.

Kahllah was perched on a stool in the kitchen, wearing one of Gucci's bathrobes. Her long black hair was wet, and hanging around her shoulders. The first thing she'd done when they got to the house was take a hot shower to wash off the stink from the men who had touched her, and their blood. For as calm and composed as she was, you'd never know that she'd nearly been raped and had killed several people only a few hours prior. She sipped hot tea from a mug, watching everything and everyone from over the rim.

Ashanti leaned against the refrigerator, drinking a beer with a confused expression on his face. He opened his mouth to say something, but a look from Kahllah silenced him. It was not the time or place for his street corner humor.

T.J. sat on Gucci's lap, with one of his books in his hand. He flipped the pages, and rattled off in gibberish acting like he was reading to his mother. Every so often, Gucci would spare him a smile or loving touch, but her attention was directed elsewhere.

Animal did his best to avoid looking at Gucci. Every time he saw the hurt in her eyes, it cut him like a knife. Thought he wasn't looking at her, he could feel Gucci watching him, her eyes burrowing into him, searching for an explanation. His dark past had seeped into her life and yanked the bottom out, yet again.

In the center of this tense moment was the impossible, Animal's past and future colliding in the middle of his living room. Fire red hair fanned out around her face, while cold gray eyes stared at him, challengingly. Sonja had gained some weight since the last time he'd seen her, but it had been distributed in all the right places . . . breasts, thighs, hips, everything was looking right. It had been years since he had seen Red Sonja, and had it been up to him he'd have lived the rest of his days without ever having seen her again, but here she was, underdressed and as belligerent as ever. Not only had Sonja popped back into the picture at the worst possible time, she brought some life altering news with her.

A little girl, with auburn hair and almond colored skin sat on the couch, half paying attention to the cartoons playing on the big-screen television. Her dark eyes watched Animal like a hawk, studying him. It must've been just as eerie for her as it was for him, each seeing their face on someone else's body. T.J. climbed from his mother's lap and waddled over to the little girl, attempting to show her something in his book. She spared him a glance then went back to watching Animal. There was a calm to her that was far beyond her few years on earth. Even if it had not been for the little girl's curly hair, and bowed lips, he would've known she was his. From the moment he'd laid eyes on her, their souls connected in a way that only those of Animal's *troubled* bloodline could've understood.

"How?" was all Animal was able to blurt out.

Sonja rolled her eyes and mock slapped her forehead. "Jesus, do we have to go through this again?"

Animal gave Sonja a look and whatever smart remark she was about to follow up with died in her throat.

"Animal," she began in a much more civilized tone, "I was as shocked as you when I found out I was pregnant with Celeste. You know how we were living out there and it didn't exactly make for the ideal environment to raise a child in. Still, it didn't change the fact that I was about to be a mother and there was nothing that I could do about it besides step to the plate and show our daughter better than we were shown."

Animal looked from the daughter he'd just met to the woman he used to sleep with. Uncertainty and suspicion was etched across his face. "You've kept quiet about her all this time, now you suddenly pop up out of the woodwork with this *Maury* shit. Why didn't you come to me sooner?"

"Because I didn't need you!" Sonja snarled. Picking up on her mother's hostility, Celeste got off the couch and moved to stand beside her, glaring at Animal angrily for having upset her mother. The soft touch of Celeste's hand in hers calmed Sonja and reminded her of why they'd come. "Animal, is there somewhere we can talk?" she cut her eyes at Gucci. "In private."

"Sonja's right. This is something we need to discuss in private and not in front of these kids," Gucci agreed.

"*We* is French and it's a safe bet that your black ass has never been anywhere near France," Sonja mocked her. "This is between me and my daughter's father. Whatever Animal chooses to share with you after the fact, he's welcome, but *this*," she motioned at herself, Animal and Celeste, "is not your business."

"Well *this*," Gucci raised her left hand, flashing the big diamond on her ring finger that Animal had brought her, "makes it my business. Sonja, it's bad enough that you have disrespected my home and my marriage with this foolishness and you think I'm going to further sit by while you go off to whisper more secrets into my husband's ear? You got me totally fucked up."

"Gucci—" Animal began, but she cut him off.

"*Gucci* my ass. I've played the naïve girlfriend through a lot of shit over the years, Tayshawn, but I'm no longer your girlfriend, I'm your wife. I need total disclosure on this one. You owe me that much."

Animal looked back and forth between Sonja, who was standing there with her arms folded, looking irritated, and Gucci, who had her arms folded, daring him to deny her. He was in a lose-lose situation. "Fine," he relented. "Kahllah," he turned to his sister, "I know you've got some pressing business to attend to and I hate to impose—"

"No, it's okay," Kahllah cut him off. "You guys go and get this sorted out. I'll keep an eye on the kids. It'll give me a chance to spend some time with my niece and nephew," she scooped T.J. in her arms. She was still sore from the beating she'd taken at Klein, but she was good at masking her pain. "Let's go, pretty girl," she extended her hand to Celeste. The child just stared at it as if she was weighing whether to bite Kahllah's fingers off or not. She was definitely Animal's kid.

"It's okay, Celeste. Go with your auntie," Sonja told her. "Maybe you can get her to tell you the story about the *Black Lotus*."

Kahllah couldn't hide her shock. Her angry eyes went from Sonja to Animal.

"Don't worry, Animal didn't spill the beans. Just know that you aren't the only one good at doing your homework on people, especially when they're *family*," Sonja gave her a wink. "Your secret is safe with me."

Kahllah wanted to leap across the room and knock every tooth out of Sonja's mouth, but for the sake of the children and helping to keep the peace, she held her composure. She had heard stories about the infamous Red Sonja, and though she hadn't known her for a few minutes, she knew that she couldn't stand her. She would let it go, for now, but if she said something else slick Red Sonja would learn the hard way that Kahllah wasn't as tolerant as Gucci when she jumped in her ass.

Animal felt much better when they were outside on the deck. In the house it felt like the walls were closing in on him. In the open space, it was easier for him to breathe. Animal slid one of the wooden chairs out from the table so that Gucci could sit, but she just rolled her eyes and instead leaned against the wall, glaring at him.

"Aren't you going to offer to pull my chair out too?" Sonja asked.

Animal kicked the chair and sent it sliding in Red Sonja's

direction. She caught it with her foot, spun it around the correct way, and sat down gracefully. Her reflexes were still as sharp as ever. "Who says chivalry is dead?" she crossed one thick leg over the other.

Animal caught himself almost staring. "What's your game Sonja?" he asked in an irritated tone.

Sonja shrugged. "It's no game. Like I told your girlfriend ☒"

"*Wife*," Gucci corrected her.

"Whatever," Sonja waved her off. "Like I was telling this broad, Celeste is your kid and it's long overdue that you two met."

"So we're just supposed to take your word for it that Celeste is Animal's?" Gucci asked.

Sonja gave Gucci a pitiful look. "You and I both know you're reaching with that one. You've seen her, and they're almost identical twins, but I do understand the mistrusting nature of hood-boogers. Every time you turn around some young bitch is trying to put a baby on a dude that doesn't want to be bothered. I dig it, and respect your suspicions, so I came baring gifts." Sonja dug in her purse and removed an envelope, which she held out to Animal.

"What is that?" Animal asked suspiciously.

"A letter bomb," Sonja joked. "Just open it."

Animal opened the envelope and removed the folded piece of paper inside. He had to read it twice to make sure his eyes weren't deceiving him. He was speechless.

"And before you ask, yes, it's authentic. You can even check out the clinic that performed the paternity test and you'll find that they're legitimate," Sonja told him. "Knowing you, I knew I'd have to come with more than my words and a pretty face to convince you, so I took the liberty of having the test done before I came to you. I figured this was less trouble, unless you guys would've rather we'd done it on the Maury show?" she cut her eyes at Gucci.

Gucci snatched the paternity test from Animal's hand and read it for herself. "This is bullshit," she balled it up and threw it at Sonja. "Where would you even get a sample of Animal's DNA to compare?"

Sonja smirked, as if she had been waiting for the question to be asked. "You must've forgotten that for the two years that you two were apart it was me who warmed Animal's bed and attended to his manly needs. We practically lived together on the compound, so it was easy enough for me to get more than what I needed from the things he left behind when he came running back to you. We can debate this all day, but it still won't change the fact that Celeste is Animal's child, same as T.J."

Animal ran his hands through his hair, grabbing two fists full of his roots and gave them a tug. Him focusing on the pain in his scalp was the only thing that was keeping him from having a meltdown and lashing out. "This is classic Red Sonja," he seethed.

"And what's that supposed to mean?" Sonja asked.

"It means let's cut the bullshit and get down to the reason you're here," Animal spat. "By my count, Celeste should be about three, which means if you were really concerned about me being in her life, you'd have reached out long before now. You ain't hurting for no bread, I doubt that's the angle," he leaned in and looked Sonja in the eyes. "Don't fuck with my heart or my patience Sonja, cut to the chase and tell me what you want."

"You think you know me, don't you?" Sonja asked in an amused tone.

"Better than you think."

Sonja tapped her manicured fingernails on the table. Animal was staring down at her triumphantly. She hated the fact that she was so transparent when it came to him. His eyes seemed to be able to look directly into her soul. "You're right, there is another reason why I've come," she admitted. Animal opened his mouth to say something, but she silenced him with a raised finger. "Before you say something that might want to make me disrespect your home, hear me out. I know you think that I came here just to be a bitch and complicate our life, but I haven't. When you left me to come back to Gucci, I respected your decision, and I still do. Had it been up to me, you'd have probably never known about Celeste, and I've have continued raising her on my own. Contrary to what you or your bitc . . . lady think, I have no designs on you."

"Then why have you come?" Animal asked.

"To call in a marker," Sonja said. "A life for a life. I gave you your life back when I helped you escape Puerto Rico, and in return I want you to take a life for me."

Animal looked at Sonja as if she had taken leave of her senses. "You must be crazy. You think you can just march in here and send me out to kill like some trained dog? That isn't my life anymore."

Sonja looked down at the blood on his boots. "Isn't it? Animal you can try to convince Gucci and everyone else that you're happy living a square's life, changing diapers and having Saturday afternoon barbecues, but I know your heart. The smell of blood makes your dick harder than I ever could. Admit it, you miss the life."

Animal was too cool to show it, but Sonja had struck a nerve. For a long time he had been trying to convince himself that he could be content, living quietly with his wife and son, but there was always a part of him that missed the smell of gun smoke and mayhem. It wasn't until he had gone on the mission with Kahllah and Ashanti that he realized how much he missed it. "Sonja, even if there was any validity in what you were saying, what makes you think I would kill for you?"

"Oh, I hold no illusions about what you would or wouldn't do for me. The fact that I laid the world at your feet and you still left made that clear. No, you wouldn't kill for me, but you would kill to protect your daughter, which is what has brought me to your doorstep."

Now she had Animal's attention. "Celeste is just a kid, why would someone be looking to harm her?"

"The man who I have come to ask you to murder, Poppito Suarez . . . my father."

#  SEVEN

FOR THE SECOND TIME THAT NIGHT, Red Sonja had managed to shock Animal. Of all the names he expected her to pull out of a hat, Poppito wasn't one of them. Poppito Suarez was not only Sonja's father; he was also the leader of a powerful drug cartel based in Old San Juan Puerto Rico. During Animal's time with the mercenary group, Los Negro Muertes, it had been Poppito who employed them. He'd hired K-Dawg and his men to eliminate one of his rivals, a dirty police captain named Herman Cruz, who stood in Poppito's way of being the undisputed ruler of the island and the drug trade. It was Animal who had dealt Cruz the death blow that secured Poppito's position. Poppito wanted to keep Animal on as a general in his new army, and Sonja's future husband, but Animal's heart wasn't with Sonja in Puerto Rico, it was with Gucci in New York. Poppito wasn't a man who took rejection well, so with the help of Red Sonja he fled the island and put that part of his life behind him, or so he'd thought.

"I don't buy it," Animal told her. "Poppito is a cruel bastard, but he worships the ground you walk on, so I can only imagine how he felt about his first granddaughter. What would make a man who places such high value on family turn on you?"

"The same thing that makes most men act out of character, a woman," Sonja said. "Quite a bit has changed since you left, Animal, including my relationship with my father. When Poppito took over it was supposed to usher in a new age for our people, but all we ended up doing was trading one devil for another. Things were good at first, but it all went sour when my father started seeing that bruja, Lilith," she spat.

Animal's Spanish was rusty, but he knew that *bruja* meant witch.

"He and Lilith met at a big party he threw for some of our cartel affiliates from Cuba," Sonja continued. "She was the special advisor to their leader, which is a nice way of saying whore. From the moment I laid eyes on her and her children, two sons and an adopted daughter, I knew they would be trouble. My father, however, fell head over heels for Lilith. Not since my mother have I ever seen him look at another woman the way he looked at Lilith. I'll spare you the details, but the short version of the story is, when the Cubans left, Lilith stayed behind with us. It didn't take long at all before that viper started whispering in my father's ear and things began to change. Not long after Lilith and her sons came to stay with us at the compound, my father took ill. Granted, he was getting on in years, but he had always been pretty fit for a man his age. As his health began to fail, he became more and more dependent on Lilith. Lilith became his voice, and even gave her sons positions in the cartel. At Lilith's suggestion, my father made her eldest son, Peter, commander of his personal security team, which didn't sit well with my brother Chris. Chris had always been the captain of my father's personal guard, and to be replaced that way hurt him. My father told him that by having Peter command his guard it would free Chris up to start learning the legal side of the business so that he could one day take over on that end. We all thought it was bullshit, but it was father's will. The longer Lilith stayed on the more influence she held over my father. It got to a point where it seemed as if he could no longer make decisions without first consulting her. Some whispered that she had cast a spell on him. At first I laughed it off, but looking back at how thing played out, there may have been some truth to it, if you believe in that sort of thing."

"So how did your father's relationship with this Lilith person lead to Celeste being in harm's way?" Animal asked.

"I'll get to that. When my father announced his plans to marry Lilith, we were all against it. Even his closest advisors advised him against it, but my father could not be swayed. Even as his concubine, Lilith had too much power over my father's affairs and as his wife her power would be solidified. The only thing we had working in our favor was a provision in my father's will that stated upon his death, his power and all his holdings would shift to my brother Chris and me, since my mother was dead."

"But if Lilith became his wife, she would be able to challenge your claim," Animal began piecing things together.

"Precisely," Sonja nodded. "Lilith had already begun planting seeds of distrust in his mind, causing him to remove men who had served him faithfully for years and replace them with soldiers of her choosing. If daddy died after he married Lilith there was no doubt in anyone's mind that the days of Poppito's old regime would be numbered. The straw that broke the camel's back was when my brother Chris was killed."

This shocked and hurt Animal. He and Chris had been friends during his days running with Los Negro Muertes. He was a young and very likeable dude who Animal had taken under his wing. "I'm sorry. How did it happen?"

"They *said* he was attacked by enemies of my father and murdered at the harbor in Old San Juan, but that's bullshit. Our family has controlled that harbor for many years. It was the heart of our empire and no one would have dared attack Chris there. The people loved him in Old San Juan. I suspect Lilith had my brother murdered."

To Animal the theory made sense if everything Sonja was saying was on the level. For as long as he'd known her, Red Sonja had been a lot of things, but a liar wasn't one of them. "Did you tell your father this?"

"Of course I did, but I may as well have been preaching to the choir. My father had his head so far up Lilith's ass that she was quickly able to punch holes in my accusation and spin him in another direction. She had convinced him that it was the work of his enemies and that they were on the cusp of another war for control of Old San Juan. She convinced my father to unite with her associates from Cuba to strengthen his empire and crush their opposition. To solidify the union, when Celeste became of age, she was to marry the young son of one of Lilith's associates. Needless to say, I told that bitch where she could stick her arranged marriage, which pissed her off. She accused me of being disloyal to my father's cause," Sonja laughed. "I gave up my nursing career and put medical school on hold to work for my father and my loyalty was being questioned."

"And what did your father say about all this?" Animal asked.

"Absolutely nothing," the pain in Sonja's voice was clear. "When my father tried to let his fiancé try to sell my child . . . his granddaughter, to strangers in the name of power, I knew he was lost to me. I could've stayed and challenged Lilith outright, but I knew if I did there was a good chance I'd have end up dead, like my brother, and there would be no one to stop Lilith from doing whatever she wanted with Celeste. So we ran, and Lilith's people have been hunting us like dogs ever since."

Animal weighed her story. Poppito was a man who wielded an immense amount of power, and if Lilith was now the puppeteer and he the puppet, Sonja and Celeste truly were in grave danger. For as airtight as her story was, there was still something about it that sounded off. "Okay, I can understand why you ran, but how does me killing your father help Celeste? You already said that his wife is controlling things now."

Sonja smiled. "Now here comes the good part. He and Lilith aren't married yet. With the death of Chris and me running off, they had to postpone the wedding. Lilith's power doesn't become absolute until my father says *I do*, and if he was to meet his end before it becomes official—"

"—by default everything goes to you as his last living heir," Animal finished her sentence for her. Now everything made sense.

Sonja clapped her hands slowly. "Give this man a cookie. Animal, for as much as I love my father, I love our daughter more. I've made my peace with the fact that my father is lost to me, I can live with that. What I can't live with is having Celeste raised like I was, in someone else's image. I won't subject her to that."

"Sonja from the bottom of my heart, I'm so sorry that this is happening to you and your daughter," Gucci said, her voice sincere. "Speaking from experience, I know what it's like to be hunted, but I can't imagine what it's like to have to live that way with a child involved. I wouldn't wish that on my worst enemy."

Sonja nodded. "Thank you."

"That being said, you can't ask this of Animal," Gucci continued. "My heart goes out to you and your baby, but what about my baby? If these people are as dangerous as you say then T.J. is going to lose his father."

"If he doesn't help, Celeste loses both her parents because I'm as good as dead and Celeste will be somewhere in Cuba." Sonja shot back. "Gucci, it's like I said, if I didn't have to come here, I wouldn't have."

"I assume your proposition comes with a plan?" Animal asked, to Gucci's surprise.

"You're not seriously considering this?" Gucci asked in disbelief. The look on his face said that he indeed planned on going through with it. She didn't know whether to scream, cry or hit Sonja over the head with a chair. Gucci tried to hold back the tears, but they fell anyway . . . one by one, tracing thin lines down her face.

Animal reached for Gucci, but she pulled away. He backed her into a corner and wrapped his arms around him. She struggled, but he wouldn't let her go. "Everything is going to be okay. I promise."

"You said you were done with this," Gucci sobbed into his chest.

"I am, ma, but I have to help her," Animal said.

"You don't owe her anything, Animal."

"You're right, I don't, but I owe it to Celeste. Gucci, you know me and my heart. If my daughter is in danger, I can't just sit by and do nothing. I won't leave her to the dogs like my parents did me. She's my blood."

Gucci wanted to argue the point. She wanted to point out the obvious, that he had a wife and son who loved and depended on him, but knowing Animal, he had already weighed it before making his decision. His nature wouldn't let him turn his former lover or their love child away, and that's what hurt Gucci the most. Someone else was intruding on what was supposed to be sacred to only her, his heart. Not able to bare it anymore, Gucci pushed away and walked out onto the beach. Animal wanted to follow, but it wouldn't help. He would allow her space.

Animal turned to Sonja. All the love and affection that had been in his eyes only a few seconds prior had bled away, leaving behind the inky coldness of a killer. "I'll do this, and after that I don't want to see or hear from you. I'll provide you with money for Celeste and arrange visitation, but other than that I don't want to hear from you, ever again."

"Fair enough," Sonja agreed.

"Now, where do we start?"

Sonja smiled. "I couldn't wait for you to ask. New York City."

This surprised Animal. "Why there? I thought you said your problem is in Old San Juan?"

"It is, but we can't just roll in there and blast my old man. Security is tighter than the president's. We're going to need some invitations, and New York is where we can pick them up."

Going back to New York was an unexpected twist and Animal wasn't sure how he felt about it. New York was a city where he had left a bunch of unfinished business, and dead bodies. They hadn't even left yet and he already regretted agreeing to aid Sonja in her fool's mission. "This isn't going to be easy, and our chances look even slimmer with it being just the two of us. We're going to more hitters."

"I got a few solid dudes I can call," Ashanti said, from the entrance to the house. He'd been so quiet that none of them had noticed him.

"How long have you been standing there?" Animal asked.

"Long enough to know that my friend needs me," Ashanti told him.

"I can't ask you to die for me, Ashanti," Animal said.

"You don't have to, big homie. I'd give my life for you because I know you'd give yours for me. I'm all in," Ashanti declared. His face was hard and war ready.

Animal nodded. "Then so be it. Now, what about these shooters you're talking about? We're about to sit at the big boy table, and I need to know that everybody rocking with us is game tested. There'll be no room for error."

"Don't even trip off it, Animal," Ashanti pulled out his phone. "I got just the right cats in mind for this."

# EIGHT

NORMALLY, HECTOR HATED WORKING IN HIS father's deli because things dragged and he hated talking to some of the people that came in and out of it. They were mostly older Hispanics, and other neighborhood transients who only shopped there when the nicer bodega across the street was closed. The same didn't apply on Saturday's. The owners of the store across the street were Jewish and didn't open on that day because of religious beliefs. On Saturday's everybody came into Hector's father's store, especially the young hood rats. Hector would trade them cigarettes or groceries for sexual favors.

That Saturday night was especially busy. A few of the neighborhood dudes and some girls were in the store stocking up on beer and other goods for the barbecue they were having in the projects across the street. Hector was in the middle of talking to a big booty black chick, negotiating a blow-job for a few pounds of cold cuts, when trouble walked in.

There were two of them; one a good-looking Black guy who wore his hair in neat cornrows to the back. He immediately drew the attention of several females who were loitering near the door. He gave them a wink before going into the beer aisle. His partner lingered near the front, looking over the assortment of candies along a rack. Long braids spilled from the folds of the dark hoodie he kept pulled tightly over his head. It shadowed most of his face, but if you looked closely you could see the ugly burn scars on the side of his face.

The men who had just come into the store gave Hector the creeps, especially the one with the scar. They hadn't done anything, but there was something about the energy they carried with them that made him uneasy. He wasn't sure what it was about the man in the hood that made him afraid, but he was about to find out.

One of the young dude's loitering in the store hovered behind the man, snickering at a joke only he knew the punch line to. The plastic cup in his hand reeked of hard alcohol.

The man in the hoodie ignored him, and continued looking over the snacks. He grabbed a Snickers bar and two packs of sunflower seeds and walked to the counter.

"Oh, you gonna act like you don't hear me, huh?" the young man followed him. "I'm talking to you, sun. Maybe if you take that hood off, you'd be able to hear me," he reached for the man's hood.

The hooded man spun, with cat-like reflexes he caught the young man's hand in mid-air. He cocked his head slightly, letting the light catch the web of scar tissue that went from his milky white eye to his jaw. It looked like someone had thrown acid on that side of his face. "Don't put your hands on me," he said in a low growl.

"Damn, what the fuck happened to you?" the young man

with the cup recoiled. Just then the handsome one came from the beer aisle. He was holding two beers, and smiling. The smile faded from his lips when he saw his brother facing off with the young man. From the calm of his face, he knew his brother wasn't *there* yet, but he was on the brink. "Everything okay over here?" he asked in a calm tone.

The hooded man looked from the drunk young man to his brother, whose eyes were pleading for him to calm down. "Yeah," he released the young man. "Everything is cool."

"Good, no harm no foul," the handsome one said, glad he was able to defuse the situation before it got nasty. He paid for the beers and handed one to his brother, before leading the way from the deli. They had just hit the door when the drunk young man decided to add insult to injury.

"Shit, I'd wanna hide my face too if I was that fucking ugly," he capped, which cause his boys and everyone else in the store to laugh.

It had just gotten nasty.

The hooded man turned and walked calmly back into the store. Slowly, and deliberately, he pulled his hood off and gave everyone a clear view of his horribly scarred face. "You don't like my face?" he smashed the beer bottle against the drunk young man's face, shattering the bottle and splattering beer on himself and everyone near them. The young man collapsed on the ground, bleeding from the shards of glass that had cut his face open. "I don't like yours either," the hooded man knelt beside him and whispered, "Now you're pretty like me."

The drunk young man's comrades surged forward, but when the handsome one pulled a big gun from his pants, it made the crowd freeze. "Which one of you niggas wanna know what that lead do?" he waved the gun back and forth. He could feel his phone vibrating in his pocket. Keeping his eyes and gun on the thugs, he retrieved it and answered. "Speak." He listened for a few minutes, while the person on the other end rattled intensely. "Cool," was his reply and he ended the call. "Play time is over, Cain," he told the hooded man, and made his way out of the deli.

Cain frowned. He hated having his fun interrupted. He reached down and snatched one of the fake diamonds from the drunk young man's ear. "Next time I take the whole ear," he told him before joining his brother outside. "Who was that, Abel?" he asked his brother once they were away from the crime scene.

"That was Ashanti. There's killing to be done."

# PART II

## WAR READY

# NINE

LILITH WAS UP AND WORKING IN HER garden early that morning. She'd always liked to get out when the day was fresh, but that day she'd ventured out earlier than usual. The sky was just starting to turn pink, and the sun had barely risen. It had been a sleepless night for her, and working in her garden always brought her peace. She took her time, examining petals and stems, while carefully plucking the different flowers and roots she needed.

She rose, holding her flower basket, and brushed the loose dirt from her nightgown. A soft breeze came through, causing the gown to cling to her so you could see the outline of her covetous body. Lilith was getting on in years, but she took care of her body. Her breasts still sat up on their own and gravity had yet to touch her ass. The only signs of her age were the small crows feet around her eyes and the streaks of grey through her long black hair. Outside of those things, she could give women half her age a run for their money. Her being such a beauty made her choice of lovers the topic of many debates.

Since she was a girl, Lilith had never been known to keep company with the most attractive or well-built men. Her lovers had always been average at best. She chose men like this because they were always intimidated by her beauty and it made them easier to manipulate. Lilith had never been concerned with what a man looked like, only what kind of influence he held or the extent of his wealth. Those were the lessons taught to her by her mother when she was a girl.

Lilith had emigrated from Cuba to America in the 1980s, during the cocaine explosion in Florida. She and her mother, like so many other refugees, settled into what back then were referred to as one of Miami's ethnic ghettos. Those were some rough and dangerous times. Lilith's mother had been a botanist in Cuba, so she was able to make money creating elixirs for those who didn't have the money or documentation to go to the hospital. It didn't make them much money, but it did put their family in good standing with the people in the neighborhood. Selling the elixirs was honest work, but it was the dishonest things that Lilith's mother was into that kept them from starving.

Lilith's mother was as skilled at playing on the hearts and desires of men as she was at making elixirs. She targeted men who were either less than attractive or on in years. They were intimidated by her beauty, therefore easier to manipulate. Lilith's mother would bleed them for whatever wealth or influence she could before moving onto the next. Lilith didn't like her mother's extracurricular activities, but her mother convinced her that the ends justified the means. They were women and would always be the underdogs, so to get ahead they had to use their wits to win the battles that their fists couldn't. Those lessons taught to her by her mother would be the bootstraps she would use to pull herself out of the ghetto and place herself into the position she currently found herself in, the bride-to-be of the most powerful man on the island.

Crossing the lawn, on her way back to the house, she greeted several of the armed men who guarded the property. They had been hand-picked and given the honor of serving as part of her lover's personal security force. Each of them would kill or die for their employer, or his lady, without giving it so much as a second thought. They were dedicated. The men waved or nodded in greeting, but none of them would dare make eye contact with the boss's sexy fiancé. It was said that she could read men's minds, and none of them wanted to let her in on their dirty thoughts. One word from Lilith could mean the difference between life or death for any of them, so they kept their heads down and did their jobs. Still, it didn't stop her from trying to entice them every chance she got. This is why she always wore her most revealing nightgowns when she made her early morning trips to the garden. To her, it was all just a deadly game.

Lilith welcomed the cold push of the air conditioners when she got in the house. The air outside was warm and sticky. She made her way into the kitchen, where the staff was already at work preparing breakfast. They said their respective "good mornings" but that was as far as their interaction with Lilith went. Most of the staff either feared her or despised her. Lilith could hear them at night, when they thought they were alone, talking about their employer's new mistress and the sway she held over him. In the most hushed of tones, some of them had even accused her of witchcraft. Lilith never let on that she was aware of their late night conversations, but every so often she would find a reason to fire a member of the staff, or worse. One of the young girls who cleaned the house had made the mistake of letting Lilith catching her rolling her eyes, after being given a task, and mysteriously disappeared. Her family held onto hope that she would turn up again one day, but Lilith didn't.

Placing her flower basket on the counter, Lilith began removing the contents and preparing them. She carefully washed all the flowers, and cut away the parts she wouldn't need. When everything was prepared, she placed her collection in a metal strainer, and dropped it in a pot of boiling water. When it was done, she poured the contents of the pot into a teakettle, which she placed on the tray, containing a plate of eggs, bacon and fluffy biscuits. Picking the tray up, Lilith mustered the biggest smile possible and went to serve her future husband his breakfast.

When Lilith entered the huge master bedroom, she found Poppito awake, but still in bed. His skin color was better, having gone from pasty white to recapturing some of its color. His eyes still carried a yellow tint, but were alert.

"Good morning, love of my life," Lilith greeted him when she entered the room. She had almost completely shed her Spanish accent, but thickened it when doing business or coddling her Poppito. He always said her voice reminded him of his mother. "How are you feeling today?"

"Better than I have in a few days," Poppito pushed himself into a sitting position. The blanket fell away, revealing the expensive silk pajamas he was wearing. At one time they had fit him nicely, but now hung loosely on his constantly deteriorating frame. Poppito had lost quite a bit of weight over the past few weeks.

"For this, I am thankful," Lilith said, placing the breakfast tray on a table. "Will you try and eat something today?" she removed the top of the breakfast tray.

The smell of the bacon wafted into Poppito's nose, and he could feel his stomach growling. The growling was replaced by a sick lurching feeling and the moment of hunger was replaced with sickness. "I don't think so. I'm sorry for putting you through the trouble of making breakfast for me but my traitorous body won't allow me to taste it."

"I will make breakfast for you every morning from today until forever, it is your wish. Severing you is what I live for, my love," Lilith said in a sincere tone. "If you can't eat, then at least drink something," she poured some of the tea she'd brewed into a teacup. "My mother used to give this to my brothers when they fell ill, and I used it for my own sons. It will bring balance back to spirit," she handed Poppito the glass.

Poppito's hands shook a bit, but he managed to take the teacup and sip from it without dropping it. "You are too good to me, my flower."

"I'm only doing my duty as your woman. We need you to get better soon. You have an empire to run and *we* have a wedding to plan."

"Yes, your special day," Poppito smiled from behind the teacup, while he took another small sip. "Fear not my love; I won't leave this world before I've had a chance to profess my love and devotion for you before God and our family. I've just had so much on my mind with Chris being killed and Sonja running off . . . ," his voice was heavy with emotion. "How could she betray me like that at such a critical time?"

"You know how these children are, my love. If we don't give them enough, we are bad parents, but if we give them too much, they become unappreciative. Look at George, I've spoiled him rotten, but he's never here when I need him. He's too busy jet-setting here and there," Lilith waved her hands dismissively. "But Peter, who has had to work for everything, is always by my side. He puts his family before his own needs."

"Peter is a good son, much like my Juan was," Poppito took another sip. The tea had settled his stomach. "Juan was a good boy . . . a good soldier. He would've made a fine leader had he not been killed. Chris was a good son too, but he was no soldier. He was never been cut out for this life and I was reluctant to force it on him, which is why it was such a blessing when Sonja came home. She wasn't Juan, but the soldiers respected her and I knew they would follow her when the time came. Now she's gone, Chris is dead and I am a sick old man. When God calls me home, who will look after what I've built? Why did my Red Sonja betray me?" the tea was kicking in and he was starting to ramble.

Lilith perched on the edge of the bed, draped her arm around Poppito's frail soldiers. "Fear not, my love. You still have a long life ahead of you, but when your time does come, know that I will make sure your empire still stands," she kissed him on the forehead lovingly, "this I can promise you."

Poppito rambled on for a few more minutes before the tea put him into a sound sleep. It would be hours before he woke again, and when he did, Lilith would be there waiting to administer another dose. Keeping him in these stupors made it easier for Lilith to operate freely, but it also came with its risks. Overmedicating him with the poison would eventually start to cause brain damage, and she needed Poppito to be somewhat functional . . . at least until after they were married and everything that he laid claim to went to her.

"Mother," a soft voice called from the doorway. Lilith looked up to find her daughter, Ophelia standing there. In spite of the heat, she wore a long blue floral dress that covered her legs and arms. Her black dreadlocks were pulled to the top of her head and fastened into a large bun. When she wore her hair like that you could better see her attractive face. Ophelia had skin the color of butterscotch, and eyes to match, with a wide nose and thick lips.

"Yes, child?"

"Peter is ready for you," Ophelia announced.

Lilith nodded. "Tell him I'll be along as soon as I put on something decent and not to start without me."

"Yes, mother," Ophelia said, but didn't move to carry out the order.

"Is there something else?" Lilith asked.

"There's been word of the rogue," Ophelia said.

"Well, don't just stand there in silence," Lilith demanded. She noticed the way Ophelia was looking at Poppito, hesitant to speak in front of him. "Don't worry about him. He's so far removed from this world right now that I could stab him and he wouldn't notice until the moment his heart stopped. You can speak freely."

"As you wish," Ophelia said softly. "News has come in of the rogue, and our attempts were thwarted again. We suffered several casualties." She braced herself for one of her mother's legendary rants, but to her surprise, she was calm. There was a look of disappointment on Lilith's face, but she was hardly as angry as Ophelia had expected her to be.

"Slippery bitch," Lilith spat. "It's my own fault, really. I should've never trusted a task so sensitive to novices. Mercenaries are so unreliable in this part of the world. Still, with the failed attempt our hand might've been tipped off which will put her on the offensive. Even cut off from all support, she's still resourceful and could present a problem. We should tighten up security until she's brought in and we can move forward with our plans with our friends across the ocean."

"Mother, let me go after her. It would be an honor for me to lay the traitor at your feet," Ophelia said.

Ophelia's loyalty warmed her mother's heart. "No," Lilith touched her face tenderly. "This battle is not yours, Little Flower," she called her by the nickname she had given her when she was first brought into the family. "I have something more important I need you to handle."

Lilith went onto instruct Ophelia on what she needed her to do. Ophelia didn't like it, but it was her mother's will and she would not disobey. "As you will," Ophelia reluctantly agreed to do as she was told, and left the room.

Lilith knew she had hurt the girl's pride by giving her what seemed like such a meaningless mission when there were so many more important things to do, but she would get over it. Part of her path to enlightenment was to learn to stop looking at tasks in terms of big or small, and appreciate the opportunity to serve, regardless of capacity. In the end she would be grateful for the lesson.

Of Lilith's three children, she was most proud of the one

who did not come from her womb. She had come into *possession* of Ophelia over a decade ago during a visit to the Midwest where she was conducting business with some men from the East Coast who fancied themselves pimps. Amongst their stable of whores was a young girl. She was a frail thing, with the saddest eyes. The girl seemed somewhat dimwitted, and rarely spoke unless she was ordered to. What the pimps did wasn't Lilith's business. She was there for the sole purpose of recruiting several girls to use as mules, but she couldn't get her mind off the girl. Lilith was no angel, but she had never abused a child and people who did sickened her. By the time Lilith's business was conducted, she had relieved the pimps of all the girls, and the men who owned them were all found murdered in a hotel room. Most of the girls went back to whatever lives they had come from before Lilith's liberation, but she kept the young girl with her. She was so small and fragile that Lilith didn't trust that she would be able to survive in the world on her own. She would raise her as the daughter she never had and mold her in her own image. In addition to a new life, Lilith also gave her a new name, Ophelia, after the character in Hamlet.

Lilith found herself with no shortage of problems to deal with and not a great amount of time to address them. What she was orchestrating would require great time and care, but time wasn't on her side. The longer they prolonged the wedding the harder it would be to execute her ultimate plan. She would have to speed things along and deal with the unexpected casualties as they came.

When Lilith emerged from the house, she was fully dressed. She'd traded in her nightgown for a sleeveless white shirt, black slacks and a large white hat to protect her from the sun, which had now fully risen. Flapping in her hand, pushing a soft breeze across her face was a beautifully decorated straw fan. She took her time, walking down the rear steps of the house, out onto the stone path leading to the ten aces of forest that surrounded the house.

Standing at the mouth of the woods, addressing several of the guards, was Lilith's eldest son, Peter. Much like the soldiers who guarded the house, Peter was dressed in a uniform consisting of fatigues and steel-toed boots. In his arms he cradled a long machine gun, and at his hip was strapped a machete. His hair was cut bald, showing off his tattooed head. A pair of devil horns went from his temples to the middle top of his skull. The soldiers listened intently as Peter instructed them in what he wanted done. When Poppito had first given Peter command of his personal guard, some of them were reluctant to follow the newcomer, but Peter quickly earned their respect and fear with his deeds on the field of battle. Peter was a fierce opponent and a master strategist. They called him The Fox because he was such a crafty opponent. Even if his enemy's forces were larger than his, Peter was always able to outthink them to gain the advantage. Before coming to join Poppito's forces he had helped topple several criminal organizations in Cuba, and then Miami. Lilith might've been the most proud of Ophelia, but it was Peter who had her heart.

When Peter saw his mother approaching, he immediately hurried over to meet her. "Good morning, mama," he kissed her on both cheeks. "I'm sorry to disturb you so early, but you insisted that you be notified as soon as they arrived."

"Yes, this is something that can't be trusted to second-hand accounts. I would look into their eyes personally," Lilith said.

Peter took his mother by the hand and led her deeper into the woods, where his men awaited him under a stand of trees. Hanging from several of the trees, by their arms, were three naked men, beaten and frightened. At one time they had been soldiers in Poppitio's army, but now they were branded traitors awaiting judgment.

Lilith walked amongst the hanging prisoners. "*Blood on the leaves . . .* " she sang, running her hand down the exposed ribs of one of the hanging soldiers. " *. . . blowing in a southern breeze,*" she gently nudged another of the hanging bodies, causing it to sway. "Strange fruit, indeed. So, these are those amongst the foolish few who still defy the words of our benefactor, Poppito?"

"Yes, we found them trying to flee the island early this morning and brought them here immediately, as you ordered," Peter said proudly.

The men hanging from the trees had been amongst those who had helped Red Sonja escape the island with Celeste. Lilith had managed to sway most of Poppito's cartel over to her side, but there were still a few who held onto old and misplaced loyalties.

One of the hanging soldiers spat at Lilith's feet. "Poppito has not spoken for himself since you arrived. We are loyal to him and his family, but we will not serve you, bruja cunt!"

Lilith stopped her pacing and looked at the man who had just disrespected her. "Brave," her hand shot out and the tips of her fingers dug into his throat, biting into his flesh, "but foolish," she twisted her hand and tore his throat out. Lilith flicked his blood from her hand as if it was nothing, and resumed her pacing between the corpses. "The problem with the men on this island, is that you're afraid of change." She stopped in front of another of the hanging soldiers, and looked him directly in the eyes. "I'm going out of my way to make sure everybody gets old, fat and rich, but you're so stuck in the old ways that you're inadvertently standing in the way of change," she drove her fingers into his chest, and stopped his heart. She moved onto the final hanging man, hand raised, fingers hooked like claws. "Change is coming; it's easier to embrace it than to fight it."

"I was only following orders," the last man pleaded.

"As you should, but it's too bad your orders came from the wrong mouth," Lilith told him before tearing his throat out. She used the shirt of the soldier standing closest to her to wipe her hands free of the blood. He dared not move a muscle until she was done. "Dump the bodies in the town square, but first remove their heads. Those you will collect and deliver to me when the sun sets. Be sure to use the back door," she ordered.

Without hesitation they moved to do as they were told.

"Son, attend me," Lilith said to Peter before heading back towards the house.

"You heard my mother. Clean this up," Peter barked at the soldiers before moving to catch up with his mother.

When Peter and Lilith were out of ear shot, one of the younger soldiers asked one of the more seasoned soldiers, "Why does she want their heads?"

The seasoned soldier gave the younger one a look. "Pray that you never find out," he whispered, making the sign of the cross over himself.

"Mother, with as lethal as you are, I sometimes wonder if you keep the guards around to actually protect you or just to give them something to do," Peter said when he caught up to Lilith. He had seen his mother kill many men, using many different methods, but every time was like the first time all over again.

"When you grow up as I did, you learn a few things along the way. I'm nothing more than an old woman who knows a few tricks, but it is you who I look to for protection, son," Lilith told him. She had trained all of her children in the art of combat, as she had been taught, but her most secret techniques she trusted only to Ophelia. Girls were far easier to train than boys.

"I live to serve you mother, unlike my less than useful siblings," Peter said, taking a dig at his brother and sister. Though he was already the favorite, it didn't stop him from always trying to compete with Peter and Ophelia for their mother's affections. "Speaking of my siblings, where is Ophelia? I'm surprised she isn't at her normal place by your side. Are George's lazy ways rubbing off on her and making her neglect her duties?"

"Not at all, your sister is still as steadfast as she's always been. I had another pressing piece of business for her to handle. By now she should be at the airstrip preparing to board her flight."

"Well, if it was important then I should've been the one to handle it for you, mama," Peter said, half pouting.

"Never fear, my son, I wouldn't deny you your glory. Your siblings will till the earth, but it will be my avenging angel who will reap the harvest."

# TEN

ANIMAL HATED FLYING. WITH A CAR, if something went wrong at least you had a chance to survive, but not with an airplane. You were miles in the air with nothing to break your fall but solid ground twenty thousand feet below. For as much as he detested flying, it was the quickest way to get from one side of the country to the other and time was of the essence.

He and Gucci's parting hadn't been a pleasant one. Animal tried to get her to understand his position, but Gucci wasn't trying to hear it. He couldn't say that he faulted her. It had to be a hard pill to swallow to have your husband's former lover come in and turn your life upside down. Animal hoped that one day she would come to understand, but even if she didn't, and he had it to do all over again, his choice would've still been the same. Gucci saw it as him running away with another woman, but he was really just trying to give Celeste the same chance that T.J. had and that all of their parents were denied.

While Sonja made their travel arrangements, Animal spent some time with T.J. and Celeste. T.J. resembled Animal and had many of his traits, but he had his mother's outgoing personality; Celeste was probably the most like Animal when it came to personality. She was very quiet and observant. It took her a while to warm up and do more than stare at him quizzically. When he finally did get her to engage him in conversation, he was pleasantly surprised at how sharp she was. Celeste spoke in nearly complete sentences, and knew a bit of this and that about everything under the sun, including Animal. She knew that he was from New York and had an older brother named Justice, who he didn't talk to anymore. For as much trash as Red Sonja talked about not needing Animal and not caring if Celeste ever knew him, she had taken the time to educate her daughter about the man who had helped create her.

What really came as a shock was her reaction to Animal's selection of music. Celeste had gotten hold of his Ipod and hit the button. Ironically the device was set on one of Animal's favorite songs, *Wild Child* by The Doors. When Celeste heard the first rifts of the guitar she went into a trance-like state. On her face was a look of deep concentration, as if she was trying to decipher the hidden message in Morrison's words. When Animal tried to take the Ipod from her, she started crying, so he let her be. For the rest of the time he was in the house, she sat in the corner listening to The Doors. She was definitely her father's child.

When it was time for them to leave for the airport, it tore Animal to pieces. He could've sat with Celeste and T.J. forever and been a happy man, but duty called. Animal, Red Sonja and Ashanti would go to New York, while Kahllah stayed behind with Gucci and the children. There was no way Animal would have the audacity to ask Gucci to watch Celeste while he was gone, so Kahllah offered so that he wouldn't have to. Animal felt better with Kahllah being there because he knew Gucci and his children would be safe.

Besides watching over Gucci, Kahllah had unfinished business in California. Someone within the Brotherhood had betrayed her, and she intended to find out who and why. Her starting point would be her contact person in California. Animal offered to delay his trip for a few days in order to help Kahllah solve the mystery, but she declined, stating that it was *Brotherhood business* and she could handle it. He knew that she could handle herself better than most men, but they'd gotten to her once, what if they got to her again and he wasn't there to intervene. Animal had no choice, but to take her word because Kahllah wasn't big on negotiating. All he could do from that point on was focus on the business at hand.

Animal wriggled in his seat, trying his best to get comfortable. He kept bending and stretching his knees, listening to the sound of his joints popping. Though he was sitting in first class, and had more than enough legroom he still felt cramped.

"You straight?" Red Sonja asked. "I know how much you hate to fly," she reminded him of their intimate connection.

"I'll be fine as soon as we're back on the ground."

"Well, maybe this will help you get through the flight," Sonja placed something in the palm of his hand.

Animal looked down at the little orange pill. "What's this?"

"Don't worry, if I wanted to kill you, poison wouldn't be my method of choice. It's just something that'll help you to relax." Sonja told him, showing him the pill bottle to prove that it was little more than a mild sedative. She knew Animal had a history of drug abuse when he was younger before she came into the picture. When he was still running with Tech he loved to sip lean and popped pills like they were candy. When he met Gucci, he had cleaned up his act and wouldn't touch anything harder than weed or alcohol. When the flight attendant came by, she grabbed two nips of scotch and handed one to Animal. "Wash it down with that and in a few minutes you'll be in a pretty place."

Animal popped the pill in his mouth and drank the scotch in one shot. It burned a bit going down, but the warm sensation mellowed him. "So, are you sure these guys will be in New York this week?"

"Yeah, I'm sure. They come once per month like clockwork to indulge in illicit vices and do mommy's dirty work, while she stays at the compound, mind fucking my daddy," Sonja said in disgust.

While they were waiting to board the plane, Sonja ran her plan down to Animal and Ashanti. As she'd said at the house, marching into Poppito's territory and putting a bullet in him wasn't going to work, so she had a plan to get them invited in. The invitation would come in the form of Lilith's youngest son, George. Unlike his brother Peter, who was dedicated to the hustle, George was dedicated to the lifestyle that came with it. He liked loud clubs, fast women and hard drugs. At any given time you could find George in a hot spot of some city, but his favorite place to party was New York. At least once per month he flew in and spent a few days partying. Sonja had it on good authority that George was currently in New York, and planned to use him in her scheme. They were going to kidnap Lilith's youngest son and use him as a bargaining chip for Sonja and Celeste's freedom. The condition would be that

Sonja would only surrender George to Poppito directly. There was no doubt in her mind that he would agree. Lilith would see to it. She loved her children more than anything, so even if she had to push Poppito there in a wheelchair, he would be in attendance to barter for the life of her son. At that meeting, Sonja would spring her trap and have Animal and Ashanti kill everyone there. The plan was a long shot, but it was all they had at the moment.

"I hope this plan of yours works," Animal said.

"It'll work; I just hope you and Ashanti are up to the task," Sonja shot back.

"Don't worry, Sonja. Your daddy and anybody who has the misfortune of being with him is going to sleep forever," Animal promised. "The sooner we handle this and make sure Celeste is safe, the sooner I can get back to my life."

Sonja laughed. "Is that what you call that, a life? Animal, how long do you think you can keep this charade up? Look, I think it's noble of you trying to be a model citizen and productive member of society, but we both know that's just a mask. Animal, you're a born fighter. Your whole life has been spent championing one cause or another. How long do you think you'll be able to sit around the house, making peanut butter sandwiches for your kid and watching reality T.V. with your wife before you shrivel and die like a forgotten house plant?"

"Whatever, Sonja. You always think you know everything." Animal turned to the window.

"I don't claim to know everything, but I do know that once a man starts down the dark road, they can deviate, but they can never truly get off."

Animal was trying his best to ignore Sonja, but she'd struck a nerve. Animal loved his family and being able to be there for them without having them in harm's way, but was it truly who he was? Every day when he woke up, he was thankful for the blessings in his life, but he always felt like there was something missing. There was emptiness in him that only seemed to be filled when he had blood on his hands. As the pills kicked in and the drowsiness crept over him he thought about Sonja's reference to the Dark Road and what put him on it.

Many years ago there had been a girl Animal was sweet on at the time named Noki, the daughter of the Japanese couple that owned the local market. Noki was Animal's first love, and his lone escape from his tortured life. Her parents frowned upon her and Animal's relationship, but it didn't stop them from sneaking off and spending time together whenever they could. One day in particular stuck out in his mind . . . it was the day everything changed.

Noki had ditched school that morning so she and Animal could catch a movie. Animal was on the Avenue, talking to a homie named Brimstone, waiting for Noki to arrive so they could head downtown to the theater. It was a tense time in the hood, with the war between the Bloods and Harlem Crips rapidly heating up. A member of the Bloods had been branded a traitor, feeding the police vital information that had caused casualties on both sides. A Crip named Gutter had decreed that he would rain death on every Blood he caught out of bounds until the traitor was handed over. Of course the homies refused. Tre was a rat, to be sure, but he was still one of theirs, so they decided they would handle the problem internally, and disregarded Gutter's threat. Back then, Animal wasn't a full banger, he was just a wannabe with hopes of initiation. His naïve mind couldn't process the threat and how real it was, but he would quickly learn the harsh reality that came with being affiliated with a gang.

That day Animal's mind wasn't on anything but meeting up with Noki. It was to be their first real date. Animal could still vividly remember how cute she looked when she arrived, dressed in her blue and white school uniform, with her silky black hair combed out neatly. She was the most beautiful thing Animal had ever seen, and then the ugliness came.

Animal had barely spotted the car before the shots rang out. To that day he wasn't sure what kind of gun they had used, but it seemed to have an endless amount of bullets. When the smoke cleared, Brimstone was dead and so was Noki. The Bloods had called Gutter's bluff, and he made them pay dearly for it. Watching Noki die violently in front of him broke Animal in a way that could never be repaired. It was her death that opened his heart to the evil that would soon fill every inch of it.

Over the course of the week after Noki's death, Animal stayed in his room. He refused to eat or talk to anyone. He simply slept and mourned Noki. A few different people came and went, but Gladiator was the only regular visitor. Gladiator was a notorious killer, and Kastro's brother. He was one of the most feared men on the streets, but seemed to have a soft spot for Animal. Each day, Gladiator would come to his room to try and get him to eat, or engage in conversation, but Animal wasn't receptive. From time to time, Gladiator would even sit and read him chapters from his favorite books, but Animal's expression never changed. He was in a dark place, and no one was sure what would bring him out of it.

One day, Gladiator came to Animal's room, intending to read him a few chapters from *War & Peace*. The room was dark, and when he went to flick the light on, nothing happened. He was just about to check the bulb in the ceiling, but Animal stopped him.

"Leave it," Animal's voice was a raspy whisper.

Gladiator turned to the sound of his voice. Animal was huddled in the dark near the window. He blended in almost perfectly with the darkness. The moon shone through the window, casting an eerie light on him. All Gladiator could make out was the silhouette of his wild hair and the faintest glint of gold in his mouth.

"What are you doing sitting in here with the lights off?" Gladiator asked.

"The darkness is soothing," Animal told him.

There was an edge to Animal's voice that made the hairs on the back of Gladiator's neck stand up. "Are you okay?"

"Tell me, if someone you loved was gunned down in front of you, would you be okay?"

"Animal, I feel your pain," Gladiator said compassionately.

Animal gave a sinister chuckle. "You couldn't possibly feel my pain, Gladiator. Nobody can feel my pain, but they will soon enough."

"Animal, those dudes who shot your lady will get theirs eventually," Gladiator assured him.

"Eventually isn't good enough. They should be dead now," Animal insisted.

"Animal, give yourself time to heal, and, if you still feel that way, then—"

"I don't need time, Gladiator. I need blood," Animal cut him off.

He slid off the bed and into the light, so Gladiator could get a good look at his face. Animal looked like a ghost of his former self, and there was a maddened look in his eyes that Gladiator knew all too well. It was the look of a man who had nothing else to lose. "The Crips killed Noki, so I'm going to kill Crips." His tone was calm and lucid.

Gladiator shook his head. "Animal, right now you're speaking from a place of hurt and anger. You ain't no killer."

"Yes, and those are the only things that I have to hold onto right now—hurt and anger," Animal said emotionally. "They went and killed her, Gladiator . . . gunned her down right in front of me, and I'm supposed to let that go?"

Gladiator didn't have an answer.

"You're right. I ain't no killer, but you are. Now I can go at this half-assed and maybe get away with it, or you can teach me how to do it the right way."

Gladiator studied Animal. He searched his eyes for any signs of the innocent kid that Tango had dropped on their doorstep, but found none. "Animal, you're a kid asking me to teach him how to commit murder."

"No, I'm a young man asking you to teach him how to survive. Don't deny me this," Animal pleaded.

Reluctantly, Gladiator agreed. "Okay, Animal. I'll grant you your revenge, but there's one condition."

"Anything," Animal assured him.

"When it's done, I'm casting you out of Hell," Gladiator informed him.

Animal was stunned. "But why? You don't have to worry

about me ever telling anyone you helped me."

"You don't get it, do you? I'm a soldier, but not a monster, and a monster is what you're asking me to become by knowingly putting blood on the hands of a child. If I'm not damned already, I surely will be after this. Every time I look at you, I'll either want to kill you or myself from the guilt of it, and that isn't good for either of us. Your exile from Hell is the price for my help."

This was an unexpected twist. Hell was the only place that had ever really felt like home to Animal, and the misfits who lived there had become his family. Kastro and Gladiator had become like his surrogate parents, and, had it not been for him, he wouldn't have made it as far as he had. The thought of leaving behind his home and family for a second time broke his heart, and he wanted to call the whole thing off, but his need for revenge overrode everything else. "I accept your terms. Let's do this shit."

"Animal . . . Animal . . . "

Coming from the dream, back to reality, was like crawling out of a tar pit. He was groggy, and his head throbbed slightly. No doubt a side affect from whatever Sonja had given him. His vision cleared slowly and he found not Gladiator standing over him, but Ashanti.

"Wake up, Blood. We home."

Animal turned his head and peeked out the airplane window. They had landed safely at JFK airport. Just beyond the runway he could see the New York City skyline. He was indeed home.

#  ELEVEN

"My home . . . she came to my home with this bullshit," Gucci said in disbelief. She was sitting at the kitchen table talking to Kahllah, and sipping Hennessy straight. Normally she would've chased it, but not that night. She needed it to get straight to her head.

After everything that had happened that night, Gucci was too wound up to sleep, so she stayed up all night. T.J. sensed something was wrong and tried to comfort her, but Gucci was numb. Celeste just sat, watching Gucci, as if she could read her mind. Gucci wondered if she could somehow pick up on her hostility towards her. Gucci understood that she was a child, and innocent, but she was still resentful of the child. Every time she looked at Celeste, it was like looking at Animal, even more so than T.J. She didn't dislike Celeste, but she hated what the child represented. She was Animal's first-born child by another woman, and Sonja would always have that over her.

Kahllah picked up the slack, tending to the kids. She made

them dinner and found a movie for them to watch until they fell asleep. Once the kids were taken care of, she dug up the bottle of Hennessy for her and Gucci. She could tell Gucci needed a compassionate ear, so she put her affairs on hold to help out for the night. They stayed up until the wee hours of the morning, sipping and talking. Initially, Gucci and Kahllah didn't get along. She thought Gucci was a spoiled bitch, who would likely get her brother killed, and Gucci thought Kahllah was a maniac. They butted heads more than a few times, but their mutual love of Animal forced them to get to know each other, and the two women ended up becoming friends. Kahllah had been a blessing in Gucci's life, and the glue that held everything together when Animal was in prison.

"I have to admit, you're a better woman than I am, Gucci, because I'd probably have done something to her," Kahllah admitted. "I don't know too much about the chick, but after the brief meeting earlier I can tell we won't be friends. Sonja is a character."

"That's putting it nicely, that bitch is a mess," Gucci said, before taking down the last bit of liquor in her glass. Without having to be asked, Kahllah refilled it from the bottle. "Did you see her march in here with them little ass shorts on and that whorish red hair? She's a typical THOT. I don't know if I'm angrier at that bitch for showing up on my doorstep, or at Animal for running up in that foreign bitch raw. God knows what he could've brought home to me! To top it off, this bitch shows up with a kid? I've put up with a lot of shit over the years dealing with Animal, but this right here is too much," Gucci said heatedly.

"Gucci, I can definitely understand why you're angry, but to Animal's credit, he didn't know. If Animal had any idea that he had a child floating around out there, you're the first person he would've told. Animal can be an efficient enough liar when he needs to be, but not to those he loves. However it happened, Celeste is here. How and why aren't the questions anymore, the question now becomes how does this affect your future with my brother?"

"What do you mean? When this is done, that bitch can take her kid and roll out the same way she rolled in. I'm not dealing with baby mama drama," Gucci said.

"Gucci, you and I both know it's not that simple. Now that Animal is aware of Celeste, he's going to want to play a role in her life."

"Oh, I'm not saying leave the little girl hanging out to dry. Of course I'm going to make sure that we send money for her," Gucci promised.

Kahllah gave her a disbelieving look. "You must not know your husband as well as you claim to. Animal went through some real bad shit as a kid, because he didn't have anybody. That's why he's such a good father to T.J. He knows what it's like for a kid to not have a dad, so do you really think he's going to limit his interaction with Celeste to just sending checks? No, he's going to want to be active in her life."

Gucci hadn't thought about that. She had been so focused on her anger in the moment that she hadn't given a lot of thought to the future. There was no doubt in her mind that what Kahllah was saying was accurate; Animal was going to want to establish a relationship with Celeste, but that also meant he would have to deal with Red Sonja. She wasn't the first random chick to wander into Animal's life, and she probably wouldn't be the last, but she was the first to ever make him stray. Granted, it had happened during the two years Gucci and Animal were separated, but it still didn't make her feel any better knowing that Animal had shared intimate moments with Sonja. Gucci had fought long and hard for Animal's heart, and Sonja presented a legitimate contender for her position. Gucci didn't believe Animal would leave her for Sonja, but her presence represented a threat.

"This is a lot to digest," Gucci said honestly.

"Heavy is the head that wears the crown," Kahllah quoted. "Things are a little crazy right now, Gucci, but you and Animal will pull through. You always do."

She was right. Gucci and Animal had stood against more than their fair share of immeasurable odds, and they always came out on top. A Love Child was a bit of a different situation than a gangster wanting you dead, but still a major obstacle. Gucci had spent a good chunk of her life waiting for Animal to sort through his demons and she honestly wasn't sure how many more years she had to waste while Animal played Russian roulette with his life. She loved Animal, but she couldn't force him to love himself. Gucci would do her part, and hold her husband down like she always did, but if things got too out of hand then she would have to do what was best for her and T.J.

"What time is it?" Gucci asked, rubbing her eyes and yawning.

Kahllah looked at her watch. "Almost six-thirty. You should probably get yourself a few hours of sleep before T.J. wakes up."

"Yeah, he's sure gonna run me ragged and I'll need all my strength," Gucci got up from the chair and stretched. She shuffled over and gave Kahllah a hug and kiss on the cheek. "Thanks for being such a good sister."

"Any time," Kahllah hugged her back. "While you're resting, I'm going to run out for a while. I should be back before you wake up, if not, I'll call. Animal left me a set of keys and the alarm codes, so I'll make sure the house is locked up tight before I go."

"Kahllah, where in God's name are you going at this hour of the morning?" Gucci asked. The look Kahllah gave her answered the question. "I sometimes forget you lead a double life."

Kahllah smirked. "Most of us lead double lives; I'm just one of the select few who aren't ashamed of it. Get some rest, sis and I'll see you in a few hours." Kahllah sat there watching as Gucci shuffled to the stairs leading to the master bedroom. Her shoulders sagged like she had the weight of the world on them. Kahllah imagined that she probably did. The heart was a delicate thing, and it didn't take much to bruise or break it. Time's like those, Kahllah was glad that she had no such attachments. She took no lover and mothered no children, so was the price for her initiation into her order. Kahllah had resigned herself to a life-time of service to the Brotherhood. This brought her back to her own set of issues.

There was no way a low-level, flesh-peddling half-gangster like Klein could've gotten the drop on Kahllah without help. She was the best of the best, which is why her services were in such high demand. A man would need a small army to take Kahllah on, and that's exactly what Klein had had. Obviously someone with knowledge of her mission had tipped him off, but the question was, who? Klein's contract was airtight, it bore the seal of the elders themselves, so it wasn't likely that the corruption started that high up the food chain. Kahn's name immediately popped into her head.

There was no love lost between Khan and Kahllah, because of their differing views on the future of the Brotherhood. They'd clashed several times at council meetings, and Kahn had never hid his resentment of Kahllah being a member of the Hand. Kahllah was one of three women who had been initiated into the Brotherhood since the order was founded, but she was the only one of the three to ever sit at the Hand's table. There were some who were uncomfortable with her wielding such power, but Kahn had been the most vocal about it. To him, women in the Brotherhood had their places, but sitting at the Hand's table wasn't one of them. If anyone had an axe to grind against Kahllah it would've been Kahn, but it didn't make sense. Kahllah rarely bothered with affairs of state, unless her vote was absolutely necessary to decide on a matter. She kept her distance from the everyday politics of the Brotherhood, and in return she was left to her own devices. Kahllah wasn't around regularly enough to challenge whatever he had been planning for the Brotherhood, so he wouldn't need her dead to do it.

If it was indeed Khan who had tried to have her killed, things were looking far graver than she thought. For as powerful as Khan's position as leader of the Hand made him, he did not have the authority to simply order a hit on Kahllah's life. She was also a member of the Hand, so certain protocols would've had to be observed. It would have to go before the Elders to make it official, but it didn't make it impossible. She doubted that the Elders would hand down a death sentence on her, without some sort of formal trial, but there was another way for Kahn to have her killed without risking being disciplined. All he would need was the burden of proof and the right people backing his play; three members of the hand and one elder. Those five votes, including Khan's, were all he needed to legitimately make an attempt on Kahllah's life. If it did indeed play out like that, it meant Khan had gone through quite a bit of trouble to have Kahllah removed from the Brotherhood, but the question was still, why?

Kahllah sighed. There was much to do, and she couldn't get it done sitting there thinking about it. She had to go on the offensive. Kahllah figured that her best plan of attack was to start at the bottom and kill her way to the top.

# TWELVE

"TOP OF THE MORNING, DETECTIVE SULLY," the old woman in the apron greeted him from behind the counter.

"Hey, Donna. How's my favorite girl this morning?" Detective Sully smiled at her, showing off his too small teeth that were heavily stained by the cheap cigars he was always chewing on. He was a chubby man, wearing a pair of off the rack slacks and a suit jacket he'd gotten from the Salvation Army. Detective Sully slid onto one of the free stools at the counter. The diner had just opened and he was the first customer, but the breakfast rush would start soon. The only people at the diner at that hour were Donna and her eldest son, Clyde.

Donna shrugged her frail shoulders. "I could complain, but who would listen?"

"I'd listen, mama," Clyde said in a slow drawl. He was six-foot-five, and well over two hundred pounds, but had the intelligence and demeanor of a ten-year-old.

"You're a good son, Clyde," Detective Sully told him.

"That he is," Donna patted her son's cheek affectionately.

"Hey Donna, how about a cup of joe and a couple of eggs, huh?"

"Coming right up," Donna said, pouring him a cup of coffee. "Come on Clyde, you can help me with Detective Sully's breakfast."

"Can I crack the eggs this time, mama? I promise I won't get no shells in them," Clyde said excitedly.

"Yes, you can crack the eggs this time, Clyde," Donna told him, leading her son through the kitchen doors.

Detective Sully sat, sipping bitter black coffee, and going through the sport's section, checking the scores from the night before. He cursed as he ran his fingers down the stat-line of the baseball games. He had lost more than he won, and the money from the few games he had won would have to go to paying off debts from the games he'd lost last week. Sully had a serious gambling problem, which is why after almost thirty years he was still busting his hump for the L.A.P.D, instead of having retired years ago. He was so far in the hole that he felt as if he'd never climb out. The only reason he hadn't swallowed a bullet yet was because he hadn't finished paying off his youngest daughter's college tuition. Of all the people he had disappointed in life, he never disappointed his kids. His wife . . . she was a different story.

Sully was about to check the lottery numbers, hoping he'd find a sliver of luck there, when someone bumped him while taking the stool next to his. Sully looked up and saw a good-looking woman wearing tight jeans and a low cut black t-shirt. She had long black hair that spilled from beneath the dark baseball cap she was wearing. A length of chain ran through the loops of her jeans in place of a belt. Covering her eyes were dark sunglasses. Sully might not have given her a second look, had it not been for the fact that it was already eighty degrees outside and she was wearing black gloves.

"Hello, Detective Sully," Kahllah greeted him, before back-handing him off the stool. She spun gracefully off the stool, and flicked her wrist, magically producing a retractable baton. From his back, Sully managed to draw his gun, but a whack from her baton sent it skidding harmlessly across the diner.

"Who are you? What do you want?" Sully asked frantically, sliding back on his elbows, trying to make it out of her reach.

"Where are my manners? Let me give you my card," Kahllah removed something from her bra and flicked it at Sully. A small dagger planted itself between Sully's legs, just missing his pri-vates. Carved into the handle of the dagger was a black lotus flower. Sully looked from the dagger to the woman and turned as white as a ghost. "From the loss of pigment in your face, I take it you know who I am and why I've come?"

"Somebody help me!" Sully yelled, scrambling away on all fours trying to get away from her.

Kahllah snatched the chain from her jeans and whipped it out at Detective Sully. One of the steel hooks bit into the flesh on the back of his thigh. "Don't run off before we've had a chance to chat," she pulled him towards her slowly. Kahllah reached down and grabbed a fist of his thinning brown hair. "My target knew I was coming and I want to know how?"

"You crazy bitch, I'm a cop! You can't just come in here and do this to me!" Detective Sully shouted.

Kahllah slapped him viciously across the face and tossed him through one of the wooden tables. She grabbed him by the collar of his cheap jacket and yanked him to his feet. "You're a fucking middle man for the Brotherhood, which means I can do whatever I want to you."

Detective Sully snickered. "Do what you like, but I'm more afraid of what the Brotherhood will do to me than what you will. Without their backing, you ain't shit but an over-qualified freelancer."

Kahllah kicked Detective Sully hard in his chest, sending him stumbling backward, but she jerked him back by the hook in his thigh before he could make contact with the wall. Sully opened his mouth to scream, but Kahllah's hands around his throat trapped the sound. She lifted him by his neck and slammed him through another table as hard as she could. The impact knocked the wind out of Sully, leaving him dazed and confused. She straddled him and placed one of her knives against his throat.

"You piece of shit, dirty pig, you think I'm playing with you?" Kahllah applied pressure to the blade and drew a trickle of blood from Detective Sully's throat. "Who altered the deal? Who wants me dead?"

"What the hell is going on out here?" Donna came out of the kitchen when she heard the noise. Her eyes got wide when she saw Kahllah with the knife to Detective Sully's throat. Her gnarled hands dipped beneath the cash register and came up holding a .45, which she aimed at Kahllah. "Last sons of bitches that came through here to rob my joint left with lead in their asses and I ain't about to have you break my streak," she said before pulling the trigger.

Kahllah rolled off Detective Sully, just in time to avoid a bullet that slammed into one of the benches along the wall. Detective Sully used the distraction as another attempt to flee, but Kahllah gave the chain a yank and dropped him back to the floor. She wrapped the end of the chain around one of the bar stools, which were bolted to the floor, while she dealt with the old lady and the gun.

"Clyde, we got burglars. Get the police on the line!" she screamed, trying to line Kahllah up in her sights.

Kahllah moved low across the room, sucking bullets and the obscenities Donna was hurling at her. This was one more thing, in an already fucked up day, that she didn't want to deal with. As she passed one of the dining tables, she grabbed a salt shaker and hurled it as hard as she could at Donna. The little glass shaker cracked Donna in the forehead, and stilling her and her big gun. She would have a hell of a headache, and a serious knot on her head when she woke up, but she would live. Kahllah was just about to turn her attention back to Detective Sully, when a much larger problem came rumbling out of the kitchen.

Clyde looked from his unconscious mother to Kahllah and let out a feral scream. He grabbed a meat cleaver from the cutting board and bounded the counter. "You killed my mama!" he roared, coming at Kahllah with the meat cleaver.

"Fuck my life," she said, taking a defensive stance against the brute. Clyde swung the cleaver with so much force that she guessed he could probably remove her head with one swing. She needed to take him down before they had a chance to test the theory. She stabbed Clyde twice in the side with the knife, hoping to slow him down, but it only seemed to anger him. Clyde went high with the cleaver, while Kahllah went low with the knife. She ducked under his strike, slicing her knife through his stomach.

Clyde staggered, blinking his eyes as if he had just awakened from a dream. He looked down at his stomach, as the layers of fat came open and freed his entrails. He tried to catch his intestines in his hands, but they slipped through is fingers and littered the floor at his feet. With a roar, Clyde charged Kahllah, intent on finishing her. Kahllah stood perfectly still, blade hanging at her side, and body tensed. When Clyde was almost on top of her, she made her move. At the last second, Kahllah sidestepped the lumbering brute and jammed her knife into the base of his skull. It was a quick and painless death. When she was done with the brute Clyde, Kahllah turned her attention back to Detective Sully. To her surprise, he had managed to dig the hook out of his leg and was limping towards the front door, leaving a trail of blood in his wake from the wound. Kahllah walked up on him slowly and grabbed him by the back of his suit jacket. "I ain't done with you," she snatched him off his feet and slid him down the countertop, breaking the cookie glass container of danishes when his skull made contact with it.

Kahllah climbed the counter, and straddled Detective Sully so he couldn't move. She picked up the steaming hot pot of coffee and held it over his face. "You're the broker who was handling the contract on Klein. Somebody stuck their dirty hands in my business, and you're going to tell me who."

"It's like you said, I'm just the broker. I deliver information from one place to another and get a fee. Any extra twists that get put on it aren't on me," Detective Sully said.

"Then who added the twists? How did Klein have the means and the knowledge to ambush me?" Kahllah demanded to know. When Detective Sully looked hesitant to talk, she doused him with a face full of the hot coffee.

"Wait . . . wait . . . " Detective Sully choked. "Look, you know how careful your organization is. I never meet the person who sends the contracts face-to-face; I give them the information and tell them where to pick the money up and they give me timeframes for when the hits will be done. I never see them and they never see me."

"Well I guess that makes you just about useless," Kahllah flicked her blade into a stabbing position, and held it over Sully's heart.

"I don't know who handled the contract, but I know where they outsourced the shooters from that tried to take you out," Detective Sully informed her.

"I'm listening," Kahllah said.

"If I tell you this, my life isn't gonna be worth shit," Detective Sully told her.

"Your life isn't worth shit now, but at least you still have it . . . for the moment. Where did the men come from who aided Klein in trying to kill me?"

"The guy you need to talk to is called Panama Black. He's the one who provided the soldiers to take you out," Detective Sully revealed.

The name didn't ring familiar at all. "Who is Panama Black and what is his connection to the Brotherhood?"

"Panama Black is an immigrant piece of shit, who was pissing on the heads of law enforcement in Florida until he popped up in California a few months ago. Him and his boys are hired guns, willing to put in work for the highest bidder. They have no real standing amongst the heavier crews, but they're a crazy fucking bunch."

"And how did this Panama Black come into the picture?" Kahllah was curious to know. She was aware that Khan wasn't above hiring mercenaries, but involving street punks in Brotherhood business was a stretch even for him.

"On my kid's life, I don't know. All I was told was that Panama Black would assist in coordinating the hit, which is what gave me the feeling that something was funny. For as many years as I've been setting up deals for the Brotherhood, they've never had anybody looking over my shoulder. After the incident with Klein got screwed up I started hearing the rumors about the Brotherhood booting you out."

Kahllah studied Sully's face for signs of deception, and reasoned that he was telling the truth, which only made her situation stranger. Who was this Panama Black and what was his connection to the Brotherhood? The Brotherhood of Blood had many different affiliate factions who they networked with, but something as sensitive as taking out the Black Lotus wouldn't have been trusted to hired help. Either Khan was slipping or there was something she was overlooking.

"Where can I find this Panama Black?" Kahllah asked.

"I don't know for sure. He's a nomad and never stays in one place for too long. Some guys associated with his crew got a social club over in Watts. I hear he's banging one of the waitresses, so that may be a good place for you to start your search," Detective Sully told her.

When Kahllah was certain she had all the information she needed, she climbed off Detective Sully.

"What about me?" Detective Sully asked.

"What about you?"

"Now that I've told you what I know, I'm sure your friends in the Brotherhood are going to be on my ass, if Panama Black doesn't get me first. I need protection. You gotta get me somewhere safe. With the kind of beef I'm gonna have, I need to be somewhere so secure that only God can touch me. You owe me that!" Detective Sully told her.

"You're absolutely right. I do owe you," Kahllah said, before snapping his neck. "Now you're in a place where no one but God can touch you," she said to his corpse before heading for the exit. She had more of a direction to go in now, but she still felt lost. She was sure it had been Khan who ordered her death, but Sully couldn't confirm it. Before she acted, she needed to be sure.

Kahllah had done enough damage for twenty-four hours. She figured it'd be best to head back to the house to check on Gucci and the kids, and get some rest. For as tired as she was, Kahllah knew sleep wouldn't come easy. Her head would be filled with the thoughts of a man named Panama Black, and how best to kill him.

# THIRTEEN

IT HAD BEEN QUITE SOME TIME SINCE Animal had set foot in New York . . . two and a half years to be exact. When he'd been released from prison he'd only stuck around long enough to get his parole transferred to California and he was gone. He'd often dreamt about what his home coming would be like, to breathe in the stale . . . post up on some random corner with his old friends trading war stories about the men they used to be. His return was supposed to be a joyous occasion, but it was not. He wasn't there to reconnect with the place of his birth. He was there to handle business.

"You okay?" Sonja asked, noticing the tense look on Animal's face.

"Yeah, I'm cool. It's just that, since I was old enough to hold a gun I've never been in the streets of New York without one. I guess I'm just feeling a little naked," Animal told her. Since they were flying to New York there was no way he could take his guns on the plane. Almost no one knew he was there so he doubted he would need a pistol any time soon, but it still felt awkward not to have one.

"Don't worry, big homie. Once we link with my peoples they'll make sure we got all the guns we need," Ashanti said proudly.

"I hope your people are reliable. I'd hate to have my baby daddy defending my honor with nothing but his dick in his hand," Sonja said smugly.

"My dick is none of your concern, Sonja. If you don't agree with the arrangements Ashanti has made for us, why don't you call your people to handle it?" Animal asked sarcastically.

Sonja replied by giving Animal the finger. They both knew that was impossible. Every resource Sonja had was connected to her father. She wasn't sure who, if anyone, she could still trust in the cartel.

"Speaking of your homies, do they understand the sensitive nature of our visit? The last thing I need is them blabbing it and having every nigga in the hood knowing I'm in town," Animal said seriously.

"I'd trust them with my life, in fact I have trusted them with my life and I'm still here to vouch for them. The twins are solid," Ashanti assured them.

As if on cue a green minivan pulled up to the curb where they were standing. Abel climbed out first, climbing from the passenger side. He walked up on Ashanti and greeted him with a warm smile and a hug. "My nigga," he patted Ashanti's back.

"Good to see you, Abel," Ashanti returned the love. Just beyond Abel, Ashanti saw Cain standing at the curb, smoking a cigarette and staring at him from beneath his hood. "What up, Cain? Show ya nigga some love!"

Cain expelled the smoke, and took measured steps towards

Ashanti. "Welcome back," he hugged Ashanti, but he didn't feel the warmth in it as he had with Abel.

Ashanti picked up on his vibe, but didn't mention it. "Fellas, let me introduce y'all to a good friend of mine," he waved Animal over. "This is Animal, Animal these are the twins, Cain and Abel."

Abel gave Animal dap, but Cain stared at him for a few seconds before shaking Animal's extended hand. Cain's skin was colder than it should've been, considering it was a warm day. Animal didn't know what disturbed him more about the young man, the scar that marked one half of his face, or the predatory stare he was giving him.

"Sup, with you?" Animal asked Cain, finally tiring of the staring contest.

"They say that you are a man who cannot be killed. Is this true?" Cain asked in way of a response.

Animal studied his face for signs of sarcasm, but found only sincerity in the question. "I reckon that I can be killed, they just haven't figured out a way to do it yet."

"Fascinating," Cain said, studying Animal. He had never met the man personally, but knew his body of work very well. A few years back he had stumbled across a crime scene. There was a crowd of people and twice as many police trying to keep them away from the corpse in front of the building. Cain had been able to slip through the crowd and steal a glance at the dead man. He had been shot multiple times, but what caught Cain's attention was his mutilated face. Someone had carved the word war in it. To Cain, it wasn't just a murder, it was a crime of rage. Whoever had done it was just like him, an angry and broken soul. Rumor had it that it was done by someone who called himself Animal and from there Cain dug up as much as he could on the phantom killer. It was a total coincidence when Cain and Ashanti became friends, and he found out Ashanti had been the protégé of Animal. Cain could sit and listen to Ashanti for hours as he told stories of capers he and Animal had pulled. Cain's love for Ashanti was genuine, but he also wanted to be closer to the myth. If Ashanti had learned from Animal, then Cain would learn from him.

"Damn, Blood, you staring at the homie like you wanna kiss him," Ashanti joked.

Cain's face became hard again. "You're a funny guy. I guess your time away from the hood has given you a sense of humor. Maybe one day I'll develop one," he said coldly. "Let me go help the lady with her bags," he walked off to assist Red Sonja.

"What's that all about?" Animal asked, picking up on the tension.

Abel shrugged. "My brother sometimes wears his heart on his sleeve. Give him some time and he'll come around. We should probably get going," he climbed back into the passenger seat.

Animal helped Sonja into the back then got in beside her. Ashanti climbed in the back row. Animal happened to look in the back of the van, where Cain was loading the bags, and saw that he was staring at Ashanti. It wasn't a hostile stare, just a black and constant one. Animal knew there was something between him and Ashanti that neither of them was speaking on. It was a situation that he would definitely watch closely.

Their first stop would be the twin's apartment. Sonja wanted to go check into the hotel, but Animal wasn't trying to hear it.

Before he did anything, he needed to arm himself. Once he had a pistol on his person, they could do whatever Sonja wanted. They were expecting to go somewhere in Harlem, but were surprised when Cain instead headed into Brooklyn.

"I didn't know y'all moved out of the hood," Ashanti was surprised. Neither Cain nor Abel had ever mentioned anything about having a new apartment.

"Shit, we had to. Can't keep dropping bodies where you lay your head. That shit'll add years on your life," Abel told him.

"Or take years off," Cain snickered from behind the wheel. He'd been otherwise quiet for the whole ride, except to offer a one word answer if someone asked him a question.

Ashanti ignored Cain's smart remark, and struck up a conversation with Abel. "So, what y'all cats been up to lately?"

"Trying to get a dollar, same as always," Abel told him.

"Y'all still out there banging them corners for King James?" Ashanti asked. King James was the head of a criminal organization that operated out of Harlem. In a few short years King James had gone from hustling crack and cocaine out of different housing projects, to gobbling up entire neighborhoods. At one point, he had been the biggest opposition to the reigning king, Shai Clark, until, with Animal's help, Ashanti brokered an uneasy truce. Ashanti had been one of his lieutenants until he went on to pursue other endeavors.

"We don't play the corners anymore. We're upper management now," Cain informed Ashanti.

This bit of news surprised Ashanti since he knew King James had never seen the twins as much more than attack dogs. "Congratulations," he said sincerely.

"Thanks, that means a lot coming from you, Ashanti," Abel

told him. "In an ironic sort of way, we have you to thank for it. When you left, there was a vacant seat at the table so King offered it to me and my brother."

"I guess you leaving wasn't such a bad thing after all," Cain remarked.

Their destination was an apartment building off of Atlantic Avenue near the Barclay's center. It was a surprisingly nice building with balconies and a doorman. Ashanti had to admit he was impressed with the upgrade by his young shooters. Cain drove the car into an underground garage and parked it in their reserved spot. He led the group to the elevator, and held the door while they all filed in. They stepped off the elevator into a carpeted hallway with a chaise lounge against the wall beneath a mounted brass mirror.

Cain and Abel had a two-bedroom apartment with a balcony that gave them a bird's eye view of the arena. The apartment was surprisingly spotless to be a bachelor pad. This was likely due to Abel being a germaphobe. Each of the twins had certain ticks about them, and Abel's was that he detested filth. The apartment was decorated in black and white furniture, with a few splashes of color thrown in here and there. A large television was mounted on the wall, which was turned to CNN twenty-four hours per day when Cain was at home. It drove Abel crazy, but it was one of his brother's quirks, so most days he watched television in his own bedroom. Overall it appeared that the twins were doing far better for themselves than they had been before Ashanti left.

"Not bad," Red Sonja admired the apartment.

"Oh, but you haven't allowed me to show you the best part," Abel took Sonja by the elbow. "May I?" he asked Animal.

Animal shrugged. "I got no claims on Sonja."

"Why are you asking him, like I don't have a mouth?" Sonja asked Abel with a fake attitude.

"Just trying to make sure I'm not stepping on anybody's toes. I mean, y'all did arrive together," Abel pointed out.

"But that doesn't mean we'll be leaving together," Sonja said mischievously, and hooked her arm in Abel's. As Abel was escorting Red Sonja across the living room, she spared a glance over her shoulder and caught Animal watching her. His face was neutral, but she could almost see the steam coming out of his ears.

"She's just trying to get under your skin," Ashanti whispered to Animal, noticing the tight set of his jaw.

"The sooner we get this business handled, the sooner I can be rid of her," Animal said.

Abel led Red Sonja to the long sofa that sat on the far side of the living room, just in front of the balcony doors. "You wanted to show me your couch?" Red Sonja said in a tone that said she clearly wasn't impressed.

"Have patience, sweetheart," Abel gave her a wink, before snatching the couch cushions back, revealing a hidden compartment that held a small arsenal of weapons. "Impressed now?"

"Very," Sonja said gleefully, looking over all the guns.

Animal and Ashanti came to join them, taking stock of their stash. Cain and Abel had everything hidden in that couch from handguns to small assault rifles. There was even a small case containing several grenades. If Animal couldn't say anything else about the twins, they were serious about their hardware.

"You boys don't fuck around do you?" Animal asked, testing the weight of a military issued .45. The cold steel felt good against his skin.

"War ready," Cain tapped the tattoo on his neck, which read the same. "Live every day like you're gonna die . . . "

" . . . But not before you take as many of your enemies with you as you can," Abel finished the sentence for him. The twins often finished each other's sentences, as if one could tell what the other was thinking.

"Take whatever you want. There's plenty more where those came from, if need be," Cain told them.

"I'm fucking with these," Sonja took two baby 9mms from the compartment. "What do you think, Animal?" she turned both guns on him. "They ain't quite your Pretty Bitches, but they'll do some damage."

"Don't point those fucking things at me," Animal shoved the guns out of his face.

"Relax, they aren't loaded," Sonja showed him the empty handles where the clips went. "You act like I don't know how to handle hard steel." She let the back of her hand brush against his crotch.

Animal grabbed Sonja by her jaws with one hand and forced her against the wall. "Let me tell you something, you manipulative little bitch; this ain't no game. For however you might feel about my relationship, it's real to me. Gucci is my wife and I'm about tired of you acting like you don't respect that fact. Now, you got my daughter in harm's way, fucking with your criminal ass family, and I'm going to do everything in my power to help y'all get out of it, but that's as far as it goes. There won't be no rekindling of old flames or trips down memory lane. This is strictly about Celeste, nothing more, nothing less. Are we clear?"

Sonja's lips parted into a smile. "You know it turns me on when you play rough," she taunted him.

Animal wasn't sure which made him angrier, her blatant disregard for anything he was saying, or the slow rising in his jeans. Emotionally, he wanted nothing to do with Red Sonja, but he'd be lying if he said he didn't still find her attractive. At one point they had shared a powerful bond and feelings like that didn't just fade away at the flip of a switch. Sonja knew it and was playing on that. Animal was so mad that had she been a man, he would've pummeled her on the spot, but that's what she wanted. Sonja didn't care if it was negative or positive attention she got from Animal, as long as she got attention.

"I ain't gonna play this game with you," Animal shoved her away and went to stand on the other side of the room.

"Ha, I knew I could still rattle that cage," Sonja laughed.

"Shorty, why don't you be cool. Provoking him isn't necessarily the smartest thing to be doing," Ashanti told her.

"Be cool, Emmanuel Lewis," Sonja patted him on the cheek. "Me and your boy been playing this love hate game for years." She sauntered off to join Cain and Abel back at the weapon's chest.

All Ashanti could do was shake his head. "Did this broad just call me Webster?"

# FOURTEEN

AFTER THE WEAPONS WERE DISTRIBUTED, ABEL CALLED for some take-out and they all got down to the business of planning the mission. Sonja was still griping about going to the hotel, but that would be wasting precious time they didn't have. It was less than twenty-four hours before they were to make their play to snatch George, and there was still a lot of preparation to be done. They had to move quick or risk losing their window of opportunity.

They were all sitting around the coffee table in the living room, going over the files that Sonja had compiled on George. It was quite an extensive collection of information. Sonja had his flight information, names and layouts of clubs he frequented, and a list of known associates in the city. She was even tracking his credit card transactions through a friend she had at the company. She had definitely done her homework.

Animal plucked up one of the many pictures of George spread out on the table and studied it. From what Sonja had told them, George fancied himself a lady's man, with a skeleton key to every woman's bedroom. Looking at him, Animal could see why. He was a handsome Cuban, with smooth dark skin, a head full of silky black hair and a smile that had to have cost him at least twenty grand. George was very easy on the eyes indeed. Listening to the change in Sonja's pitch every time she said George's name made Animal wonder had George ever found his way into her bedroom before things went sour.

"Who's that?" Cain asked, pointing at another photograph on the table. This one was of George and another man. He and George had the same smooth dark skin, but that's where their similarities ended. He had a hard face and wore his hair cut close to his scalp, showing off the devil horns tattooed onto his skull.

"That's George's older brother, Peter," Sonja told him. "Since they moved in, Peter has barely left the compound. Being too far away from his mother takes him out of his comfort zone, so he plays her close."

"Ha, a mama's boy!" Abel laughed.

"Yes, Peter is a mama's boy, but he's also a stone cold killer. If he'd been here with George I wouldn't have even suggested we try this tonight," Sonja admitted.

"Then I guess we should count our blessings," Ashanti said.

"Fuck counting blessings, let's count how many bullets we're gonna put in this dude when we ride down on him," Cain added.

"The plan is to take him alive, not kill him. He's no good to us dead," Animal told Cain.

Cain looked disappointed. He was an executioner, not a kidnapper. Violence was his element and it put him in a funk whenever he had his heart set on it and was denied.

"Buck up, youngster. I'm sure you'll get your share of action before the night is over," Sonja told him. "George usually travels with a small security team, never more than two or three men. Unlike his brother, he's never been comfortable moving with large entourages, so he keeps his numbers small to fly under the radar."

"Two or three guys shouldn't be too hard to take out to get to him," Ashanti said.

"Don't be too overconfident, Ashanti. What George's entourage lacks in size, they make up for in skill. These aren't just some street corner punks, they're trained killers," Sonja told him.

"So are we," Cain said confidently.

"Solid," Abel extended his fist.

"Solid," Cain pounded Abel's fist.

Sonja smirked. "I think I like you two. Maybe if you don't get your little cocky asses killed before its all said and done, we can have some kicks."

"The plan, Sonja," Animal reminded her.

"Right, the plan," Sonja went back to her files. She shuffled some papers until she found the small blueprint she was looking for. "George will be partying at this spot tonight," she tapped the blueprint with a manicured red nail. "It's a high end joint down in midtown that he's fond of. You take him down inside the club, and drag his ass out before anybody gets wise."

"Why not just wait until he comes out and take him then? He'll probably be fall down drunk and easy pickings," Abel pointed out.

"I'd already thought of that," Sonja informed him. "We have

to catch George at a vulnerable point and get him under wraps before anybody gets wise. George will probably be half out of it, but his security will be on point. Most times when shit goes down at clubs, it happens outside when the club is letting out. They'll be more relaxed inside the club, because they figure the chances are less likely someone will try something stupid out in public."

"Then they must not know us, because we're surely about to do some stupid shit," Animal half joked.

"But you're doing it for a good cause," Sonja reminded him. "Now, I have a friend that works in the kitchen who is going to make sure you guys can get in with your guns. Cain and I will be outside with a car waiting, while you and Ashanti and Abel go in and bring George out."

Cain frowned. "Sit in the car? Nah, if my homies ride, I ride. Who says I gotta sit in the car and play the background?"

"That beauty mark of yours says so," Sonja pointed at the scar. "You've got a face too easy to trace and George knows me on sight so I can't go in. The element of surprise is the only thing we have on our side right now and we can't lose that because you want your pound of flesh."

Cain knew that Sonja had a point, but he still didn't like it. "Fine," he said with an attitude. "Let me know when y'all are ready to roll out," he walked out onto the balcony.

"What the hell has gotten into him lately?" Ashanti asked Abel once Cain was out of earshot.

Abel gave Ashanti a knowing look. "Do you really need to ask?"

"I'll talk to him," Ashanti promised.

"You might want to. The longer this shit festers the worse

it's gonna get. Y'all make this shit right so we can get things back to the way they were," Abel said.

"I got you," Ashanti said and followed Cain out onto the balcony.

"I need to make a call. Is there some place quiet that I can use?" Animal asked Abel.

"Yeah, you can go in my bedroom. Go down the hall and it's the first door on the right," Abel directed him. "Well, looks like it's just you and me, beautiful," he said to Sonja after Animal had gone. He had been flirting since she'd gotten there and was ready to make his play.

Sonja saw the bitch long before Abel threw it. "You're cute, and if you're lucky enough to live into your twenties, you might go on to be something special, but for right now, you're still a pup. For a chick like me, it's the top dog or nothing," she said, with her eyes looking toward the bedroom where Animal had disappeared to.

Animal sat on the edge of Abel's king-sized bed, staring down at his phone and breathing heavily through his nose. His grip on the phone was so tight that he could hear the plastic begin to crack. He had to check himself. His cell phone was his only connection to the life he'd put on hold in California and if he broke it he'd feel even more alienated than he already did.

He'd been trying to call Gucci since he arrived in New York, but kept getting her voice mail. For a minute he thought something was wrong and was about to call Kahllah, but he was finally able to reach Gucci after the tenth attempt. From the tone of her voice he could tell that he was still in the dog house. Animal told Gucci they'd arrived in New York safely and inquired about things in the house and the kids. Gucci let him know that everything was fine, but other than that she didn't have much to say. The conversation was one sided and filled with a lot of uncomfortable silence. He started to ask to speak to T.J. and Celeste, but decided against it. Hearing his children's voices would've only reminded him of how much he'd have rather been home, instead of in New York, about to commit a crime. He needed to keep his head in the game. When Animal tried again to broach the subject of why he was doing what he was dong, Gucci told him to go fuck himself and ended the call. He hadn't been able to reach her since.

Animal felt a hand on his shoulder, which startled him. He jumped from the bed, hands raised and ready to defend himself, when he saw Sonja standing there.

"There was a time when it would've been impossible to sneak up on you," Red Sonja said.

"I've got a lot on my mind," Animal told her.

"And that's exactly my point, you're distracted. I don't have to tell you that in our line of work, allowing yourself to be distracted is the quickest way to get yourself murdered."

"There ain't no *our line of work* for me anymore, Sonja. This is one job and I'm done," Animal assured her.

"So you say. If you get killed before the job is done then you'll no longer have the choice."

"You mean like when you had the choice to tell me about Celeste when you found out that you were pregnant, or waiting three years later to drop it on me and completely changing the dynamics of my life?" Animal shot back.

Sonja's eyes narrowed to slits. "You always were good at using your words like fists when you wanted to hurt me. Okay, you're right. I should've told you about Celeste, but could you blame me for not telling you? To be honest with you, I wasn't even sure that I was going to keep Celeste. The last thing I wanted to do was bring a child into the lifestyle we were living in Old San Juan, especially without a father. When you left, you made it clear that you didn't want anything to do with me. If I had popped up talking some baby mama shit, it'd have looked like a desperate attempt to hold onto something that didn't want to be kept, much like last night when I showed up at your house."

"Sonja, you know me better than that. Regardless of how things played out with us, if I had known about Celeste, I wouldn't have left you to raise her on your own," Animal said sincerely. "A man can still be a good father without being in a relationship with her mother."

"I know, Animal. Deep down, that's part of the reason why I never reached out," Sonja confessed. "You have to remember that when you came back to New York, you dove head-first into a blood feud. Every other day it seemed like somebody different wanted to blow your head off. I was trying to protect Celeste from the violence, and allowing you into her life would've thrust her further into the fire. I'm not trying to say that I was right in the way I handled things, but I was just doing what I thought was best for my daughter."

"*Our* daughter," Animal corrected her.

"Right . . . *our* daughter. Animal, I know you probably hate me for putting you in this position, especially with the way everything came out, and I'm sorry for that, but put yourself in my stilettos for a minute. I'm literally trying to make something out of nothing for me and Celeste. My brother is gone, my father has disowned me. I'm flat on my ass, and living from pillar to post trying to keep my daughter from falling into the hands of a crazy Cuba witch who thinks we're still living in the dark ages. For the past few weeks we've been huddled up in cheap motels, scared to death to step outside for fear of my father's men swooping down on us. Me, I'm a survivor, so I can make the best out of the worse situations, but what about Celeste? How fair is that to her? Why should Celeste have anything less than a happy life because she comes from fucked up genes?"

"We're gonna get this business straightened out and you and Celeste are going to be okay," Animal tried to reassure her.

"Maybe, maybe not, but why should it even be a conversation? Animal, we've both played the odds with our lives, but ours were conscious decisions, Celeste didn't ask for this." Tears rimmed her eyes.

For as long as Animal had known Red Sonja, she had always been strong and defiant, but he saw none of those things in the woman standing before him. She looked weak, and broken, and he couldn't say that he blamed her. Animal hadn't known Celeste long, but she was still the fruit of his loins, so a part of him shared the weight Sonja felt, as well as her uncertainty. As a parent, all you ever wanted to do was protect your child against any and all odds. Just the thought of someone wanting to hurt your child could be nerve racking, but for the threat to be as real as it was with Celeste put you in a completely different headspace. Without even realizing Animal had his arms around Sonja. It wasn't a lover's embrace, more of the way you would console a family member who had just gone through something and you wanted to help ease their pain.

Sonja looked up at him, steel grey eyes flushed and red. "Why do my fights for the things I want always have to be the hardest?"

"Life doesn't throw anything at us that we aren't built to handle. You'll get through this, Sonja . . . *we'll* get through this."

Animal looked down at Red Sonja as if he could read her mind. She knew that if no one else understood what she was going through, Animal did. He knew her in ways that no man ever had or ever would. For a few long moments the two of them just stood there, enjoying the comfort of each other's arms. For a minute it felt like old times and if only for a fleeting moment their souls connected again. Their tender moment was broken up by the sound of shattering glass.

"Can I smoke with you, Blood?" Ashanti approached Cain on the balcony. Cain expelled the smoke from his nose, glaring at Ashanti as if he was weighing it. Eventually he handed him the blunt.

Ashanti and Cain stood shoulder to shoulder, smoking in silence and looking out at the city. Ashanti could see the conflict raging in Cain's face. There was a lot he wanted to say, but he knew that his friend wasn't good with words so he broke the silence.

"You got something you wanna say to me?" Ashanti asked.

Cain looked at him. "Am I that transparent?"

"Only to those who know you," Ashanti tried to pass the blunt back, but Cain declined. "Cain, what's your problem?

Ever since I got here, you've been acting like I kicked your dog."

"You gotta forgive me if your presence hasn't cause me to bubble over with joy as it has my brother, but I'm still on the fence about how I feel about you being here, especially since you cut out on us when we needed you the most," Cain said.

"Is that what this is about, me traveling with Kahllah?"

"Nah, you're grown and free to go where you please, but a nigga like me, when I'm dedicated to something, I stick it out to the end. I don't go flying around the world when my homies are dying in the streets," Cain spat.

"Cain, homies been dying in the streets long before me and they'll continue dying in the streets long after I'm gone. It's the natural order of things. I been putting in work since I was barely old enough to hold a gun. I've earned my stripes. If I wanna go out and explore other avenues of income it's my right. I don't owe the hood anything."

"Fuck the hood, what about us?" Cain asked heatedly. "Ashanti, you brought us into this shit, got us balls deep in these streets then you just cut out. You left us for dead . . . left me for dead."

And there it was. Cain looked at Ashanti like a big brother and leaned heavily on his guidance. When Ashanti started removing himself from the day to day hustle of the hood, Cain felt lost. Ashanti was still active in King James's operation, but he wasn't on the streets like he had been. If he wasn't on one of his secret missions with Kahllah, he was off doing something with Fatima. Cain tried to understand, but he couldn't. He was like the loyal dog whose owner didn't pet him as often anymore and it hurt him.

"Left you for dead?" Ashanti was baffled by the accusation. "My nigga, I gave you the game and a way to feed yourself. Yeah, I gave you an opportunity, but what you do with it is on you. Now, I know you in your little feelings and shit, but you need to suck it up and stop crying about what I didn't do for you and appreciate what I did do. I'm surprised this is coming from you because I didn't raise you to be a crying ass nigga."

"Watch how you talk to me, Ashanti," Cain warned. "I'm not a kid anymore, begging to ride out on a mission. I'm a man now."

"If you're a man then act like it, because right now you sounding like a little bitch," Ashanti shot back.

In a totally unexpected turn of events, Cain punched Ashanti in the face. Before Ashanti could recover, Cain had scooped him by the legs and hurled him through the balcony door and into the apartment.

"Aw shit," Abel cursed, when he discovered Ashanti lying in a pile of glass in the middle of his living room. Cain came stalked in a few seconds later, with a murderous look in his eyes. "Fall back, Cain." Abel grabbed his brother.

"Fuck that. Y'all wanted me to get it off my chest, so I am," Cain struggled.

"Nah, don't hold him back," Ashanti was getting back to his feet. He touched his face and his fingers came away bloody. "You wanna dance, young nigga, let's dance." He took a defensive stance.

Abel didn't want it to go down, but he knew that getting it out of their systems was the only way to make peace. He moved the coffee table and anything else breakable out of the way, and stood aside to let them scrap it out.

Animal was shocked when he came into the living room to find Ashanti and Cain duking it out in the middle of the floor. He rushed to break it up, but Abel grabbed him.

"What are you doing? If we don't break it up they'll kill each other," Animal told Abel.

"No, if we try and break it up and not let them finally put this shit to bed they'll kill each other. This has been a long time coming, let them get it out once and for all," Abel told him.

Ashanti and Cain went at each other like two rabid dogs, exchanging punches. Cain was a good fighter, but Ashanti was older and had more experience. While Cain's blows were wild and feral, Ashanti's were timed. He would let Cain punch himself out then deliver a well-placed blow. Not being able to penetrate Ashanti's defenses infuriated Cain, so he rushed him, which Ashanti had been expecting. He moved, shoving Cain as he passed, and let his momentum carry him into the bookcase. Ashanti was attempting to wrap his arm around Cain's neck to put him in the sleeper hold, when he felt Cain's teeth sink into the meat of his forearm.

"Aw shit," Ashanti rained blows on Cain's head until he let him go. He took a minute to examine his arm. There were deep teeth marks in it, but Cain hadn't broken the skin. "I can't believe you bit me! That was some dirty shit."

Cain snickered. "Ain't no rules in a street fight. You taught me that, remember? That was just a nibble; I didn't even break the skin. Now quit crying like a little bitch and let's get to it," he moved in and attacked Ashanti.

Animal wasn't sure how long they had been fighting, but it felt like forever. Both Ashanti and Cain were breathing heavy, and dragging their feet. After a while it got to a point where neither of them were even trying to defend themselves anymore, they were just exchanging punches to the face. They were both exhausted, but neither would quit. They grabbed each other around the shoulders and began tussling.

"Quit Cain, I don't wanna hurt you," Ashanti heaved, barely able to keep his grip on Cain.

"Nope," Cain said, trying his best to keep his legs under him. He was dead tired, but determined.

It was obvious that they would both have kept fighting until one of them died from exhaustion, so Animal and Abel decided it was enough, and broke it up. Ashanti took a step back towards Cain, but Animal held him.

"Let it go," Animal told him.

"It's over, Blood. I ain't gonna swing on the homie," Ashanti promised. Animal waited until he was sure he would keep his word then let him pass. Cain got his second wind and advanced on Ashanti hostilely. Abel went to intervene, but Ashanti waved him off. "I ain't gonna fight you no more, Cain. If you got more you need to get off your chest, then handle it, but I ain't gonna fight you."

Cain raised his fist, but the blow never fell. Instead he dropped his arms to his side and let out a deep sigh. "I needed you and you weren't there, Ashanti . . . you weren't there."

"Cain, I always have been and always will be there. We're more than homies, we're brothers and that's a lifetime commitment. Sometimes you need a change of pace to keep you from going nuts. I know you don't understand right now, but when you've been out her for a while longer, you will. Now let's put this behind us and get back to being family." Ashanti extended his hand.

Cain just glared at Ashanti's hand, breathing heavy. He was still angry, but more at himself than Ashanti. He'd let his emotions get the best of him. Cain slapped Ashanti's hand away, and everybody thought they were going to fight again, but instead Cain hugged him.

"If you kids are done kissing and making up, we've got a kidnapping to finish planning," Sonja said.

Animal looked at her and shook his head. It amazed him how she could go from an emotional wreck one minute to her regular, hard as nails self. Sonja had the ability to change from a porn star in the bedroom to a cold-blooded killer in the streets in the blink of an eye. She was always in control. These were the qualities about her that attracted Animal in the first place and the very reasons he needed to put distance between them as soon as possible.

#  FIFTEEN

KAHLLAH WAS NEARLY ASLEEP ON HER FEET by the time she got back to the house. Her body was tired from the round robin of ass kicking she'd been doing, but her mind was also tired from trying to unravel the mystery that had her trapped like a fly in a spider's web. The more she struggled to solve it, the more the web tightened around her. There were so many variables, so many unknowns. This was truly one of her most complicated assignments.

She crept upstairs to check on the kids, and found them sound asleep in T.J.'s bed, where she'd left them. T.J. was stretched out, with his mouth open, snoring like a grown man. Celeste lay on the other side of him. Her brow twitched, and she tossed and turned restlessly. Even in her dreams, her life was a constant fight. Kahllah felt bad for Celeste, because of all she was going through. She was no stranger to a turbulent child-hood. It was the things she endured as a kid that shaped her into the woman she had become, which could've been taken as a compliment or an insult, depending on who you asked.

Kahllah covered the kids with the blanket, kissed them both on the foreheads and crept out.

Kahllah went downstairs to check on Gucci next. She listened to the door and didn't hear anything, so she assumed Gucci had finally gone to sleep. She had been through a lot already and would likely be asked to endure more before it was all said and done. Kahllah knew that Gucci loved Animal and would ride for him against all odds, but she often wondered if she understood the magnitude of what they were facing. Though she wouldn't admit it, she was worried to death about her and Animal. Poppito was a dangerous foe, and even as thorough as the band of killers was who Animal was leading against him, they would still need an act of God if they hoped to stand even the slimmest chance of winning the coming battle.

Kahllah had considered reaching out to the Brotherhood for assistance, but that wouldn't have been the wisest course of action, considering she had no idea what her standing was in the order at that point. She was sure that there were still members of the Brotherhood who would support her, but to aid Kahllah would be to go against Khan and whoever else he enlisted in his coupe. No, she was on her own until she could figure out who was playing for which side.

Kahllah sat on the couch and kicked her shoes off. She'd intended on watching the news for a while before going to bed, but within five minutes of her ass hitting the plush sofa, she was fast asleep.

Kahllah's sleep was anything but peaceful. She had been plagued with nightmares since she closed her eyes. The last one was the most intense. She dreamt that she was a young girl again, back at the hovel the slavers kept the girls in. She was curled up on a dirty cot, listening to the screams of the girl being raped in the next room. That night, just as every night she was there, she prayed for death, but it never came. A few minutes later, her door creaked open and several men walked in. It was her turn to be conditioned, as they called it. They wanted their girls to be tight for their clients, but not too tight, so they broke some of the fresher ones in. Kahllah had been a virgin at the time.

She fought the men with everything she had but there were too many of them. Two of them bound her arms to the bed, while a third forced her legs open. Kahllah pleaded for mercy, but she knew that mercy was a foreign concept to these men. When he forced himself inside her, Kahllah felt like she had just been ripped in half. The first man did his business and freed his seed inside of her, before moving aside to let the next man have a go. Kahllah lay there, by now numb to the pain, and detached, while the men dripped sweat onto her frail body. She could still feel their rough mouths fighting to suckle her underdeveloped breasts. She wanted nothing more than to cry, but would not give the rapists the satisfaction.

There was a crash coming from somewhere behind them. Kahllah's vision was blocked by the man who was on top of her. There was shouting, followed by the retort of guns. Blood was everywhere, including in Kahllah's eyes. She tried to rub them clean, but it only made the blood seem to stick. She could feel herself being snatched from the bed and the wind whipping past her face like she was falling from a rooftop. She closed her eyes, waiting for the impact of the ground below, but it never came. When she opened her eyes, she was no longer at the hovel, but in a church.

She was older now, maybe about thirteen. She was wearing a pretty white dress and white Mary Jane shoes. She was on her knees before an altar, but she wasn't worshipping. Her arms were spread and tied to it. She struggled against the leather straps, but was no match for them.

*"The enemies of God are the enemies of his sword."* She could hear someone behind her in the dream saying. *"Those who would stand against the one true God, must be made to feel the sting of his blade."*

Fire shot through Kahllah's back as a whip was brought down across it. Blood now stained the arms of her pretty white dress and her back throbbed, but she knew that was only the beginning. It only hurt in the beginning.

*"The will of God is the only law."* The voice continued, *"Man has been corrupted and the wrong must be righted. Who has been chosen for this?"*

"The sword," Kahllah could hear herself say in the dream. "The sword must cut the weeds so that the wheat may grow." Another blow fell across her back, but she refused to scream out.

*"And it is the sword who has taken the sacred oath,"* the voice continued. *"It is the sword who has spoken the words before God and pledged to put the needs of man and the lord in front of their own. Speak the words!"*

Kahllah lips moved but she couldn't speak. What were the words?

Another crack of the whip landed across her back. This one was so intense she felt like it had taken off her skin. She felt a strong hand grab a fist full of her hair and lifted her head. Kahllah still couldn't see who it was speaking to her, but she could smell him. He wore the unmistakable smell of death like a designer fragrance. She could feel the cold touch of steel from the blade that was now pressed into her neck. *"Only the evil cannot speak the words. And as decreed by my lord and savior, the evil must be purified by blood and steel."*

Kahllah was startled awake by T.J. jumping on the couch. Her brain was still clouded by the heavy fog of sleep, so she reacted more by instinct than thought. Moving lightening quick, she was on her feet and had the little boy gripped about the arm. His happy expression was placed by a terrified one and he started crying.

Celeste appeared at Kahllah's side and began tugging at her wrist, trying to free her little brother. She bared her teeth like she was going to bite Kahllah if she didn't release T.J. The little girl was naturally protective, just like her father.

Kahllah took him lovingly in her arms and rocked him. "Auntie is sorry, T.J., you just scared me. See, I'm not going to hurt him, Celeste," she tried to assure the little girl, but she looked less than convinced.

Hearing her son crying, Gucci came flying out of the kitchen. "What's going on? I heard T.J. crying."

"It's my fault, Gucci. We kinda scared each other," Kahllah told her.

"Did he wake you up? I'm so sorry, Kahllah. I told this boy to let you sleep. I know you had a long night and you needed the rest," Gucci took T.J. from Kahllah.

"It's cool. I needed to get up anyway," Kahllah stretched. "Any word from Animal?"

"Yeah, I spoke to him. They made it to New York safely, but

I didn't want to hear anything else he had to say, so I banged it on his ass," Gucci said.

"Gucci, you need to stop acting like that. You know all Animal wants to do is the right thing," Kahllah explained.

"Staying at home with his family would've been doing the right thing," Gucci fired back.

Kahllah shook her head. "As usual, there's no arguing with your stubborn ass." She got up and went to the bathroom to clean up and change clothes.

Gucci went about the task of making breakfast for the kids. She scrambled up a couple of eggs and fried them some bacon. She wasn't sure if Celeste ate pork or not, but for as long as she was under her roof she would eat whatever they had. She placed two snack trays with the food on it in front of the kids who were sitting on the couch. For a minute Celeste just stared at the food, as if she was afraid that it might've been poisoned. She picked up a piece of bacon, examined it, before taking a small bite. Her eyes lit up when she tasted the perfectly cooked strip of pork.

"Thank you," Celeste said, which surprised Gucci. The little girl had been silent for so long that it never even occurred to Gucci that she could actually talk. Her voice was small and soft, but had the same scratchy edge to it that Animal's did. Hearing her voice put Gucci in her feelings again and she needed to excuse herself.

Gucci went into the kitchen and braced her hands against the sink, taking slow deep breaths. She felt like she was on the verge of a panic attack. Gucci was a ball of emotion. She had so many thoughts running around in her head that she felt like it would explode if she didn't get them out. Kahllah had been a rock during Gucci's hard times, and she was always willing to listen when Gucci needed to talk, but Gucci and Kahllah had only known each other a few years. She didn't know Gucci like most people did. Times like that she missed being able to get on the phone with Tionna and vent, but those days were long gone. Tionna was no longer with them and her kids were orphans, and Gucci couldn't help but feel partially to blame.

It was right after she'd gotten out of surgery. Gucci had been the recipient of a stray bullet that was meant for someone else, and it almost killed her. For a while it was touch and go, and no one was sure if she was going to make it or not, but Gucci had always been a fighter. After several surgeries and round the clock prayers by her family, Gucci was out of surgery and in her room recovering.

Unbeknownst to Gucci, while she was in recovery, Animal had come back to New York and was waging a personal war on the streets against those responsible for her being shot. In an attempt to get to Animal, his enemies came for her. Tionna had walked into the hospital room in time to discover two men putting something in Gucci's IV. The men held Gucci and Tionna at gunpoint, demanding that Gucci get on the phone and call Animal. They were laying a trap for Gucci to set Animal up, and she refused . . . but Tionna didn't. She was willing to sacrifice Animal to save her own life.

At the time, Gucci had been mad at Tionna. They had grown up like sisters and the fact that she was willing to betray the man Gucci loved, cut like a knife. It wasn't until she had T.J. and became a mother herself that she was able to better understand Tionna's thinking. Animal was Gucci's man and Tionna had no such attachments to him. She had two small kids to take care of and so she did what she had to do to keep them from being motherless, but unfortunately it didn't work out quite the way she'd planned it.

There was a heated exchange on the phone between Animal and the man Gucci would later learn was named Angelo. Gucci couldn't hear what Animal was saying on the other end, but from the angry expression on Angelo's face she knew it wasn't going well. She was afraid for Animal, but also afraid of what they might do to her if things took a turn for the worse, which they did.

Angelo had tired of Animal's defiant attitude and intended to show him who was really in charge. "You still think you're calling the shots, huh?" Gucci heard him ask, before putting the phone on speaker. "You listening, li'l fella?"

"What're you playing at?" Gucci could hear Animal's voice come over the speaker. He was nervous.

"I ain't playing at shit," Angelo told him. "I'm actually quite serious, and I'm about to show you how serious I am. Ayo," Angelo called to his henchman, "since these bitches think they're so fly, let's see if they got wings."

Gucci watched the henchmen drag the kicking and screaming Tionna across the floor to the hospital room window. Gucci knew what was about to happen, but her brain still hadn't accepted it. "Please don't!" Gucci called out frantically.

Hearing her voice made Animal panic. "Don't you do it!" Animal pleaded on the other end of the phone.

"You wanna roll with the big dogs, then you need to know how it feels to get bit," Angelo spat venomously at the phone. "Do that bitch!" he ordered his henchman.

"You ain't gotta do this!" Tionna clung to the henchman for dear life.

"Sorry, shorty. I got my orders." He took a step back and kicked Tionna as hard as he could, sending her through the window like a battering ram and into the cool night air.

Gucci had never felt more helpless than the day she witnessed Tionna's murder. She had always known that dealing with Animal wasn't without risks, but seeing Tionna go out that window brought everything into perspective. Thinking of her friend made Gucci weep. Gucci reasoned that Tionna was wrong for being willing to give up Animal, but had it not been for trying to be a good friend to Gucci she'd have never had to be in a position to make the choice.

The hot shower helped to wake Kahllah up fully and wash the soot off her from the night before. She had a busy day, and possibly night, ahead of her and she wanted to get the ball rolling.

For her hunt for the notorious Panama Black she would employ a different tactic. Instead of jeans and combat boots, she opted for a pair of tight fitting hot-pants, black stiletto booties and a leather jacket that hugged her frame. It wasn't what Kahllah would've normally worn, but for different prey you had to set the traps with different bait. For as restricting as the outfit might've looked, Kahllah was able to move quite freely in it. The weather was a bit warm for the jacket, but it was the only thing she had that would hide the weapon's harness strapped to her body.

When she came back out, she found Gucci in the kitchen washing dishes, while T.J. and Celeste were sitting in front of the T.V. eating breakfast. One of the characters on the show they were watching said something funny, which made Celeste laugh. It was the first time she had seen the child do anything other than scowl since she had arrived. Celeste was young but smart and Kahllah was sure she'd picked up on the fact that there was something going on. It seemed a crime for a child so young to have to endure so much. Kahllah knew first-hand the lasting affects of stolen innocence. She just hoped her brother got everything sorted out soon so that Celeste could go back to living a normal life, but she reasoned growing up with Red Sonja as a mother was probably anything but normal.

"You want something to eat?" Gucci asked over her shoulder when Kahllah entered the kitchen. She didn't want her to know that she'd been crying.

"Nah, I'll probably grab something when I hit the streets," Kahllah told her, taking a seat on one of the stools.

Gucci wiped her face with a paper towel and turned to Kahllah. "Kahllah, do you ever stop moving?"

"Not really. I like to keep busy. Idle time is a tool of the devil."

"Idle time isn't the only thing that's a tool of the devil," Gucci nodded to the harness peeking out from beneath Kahllah's jacket. Knowing Kahllah it was probably packed with all sorts of hidden goodies. "You and Animal might not be related by blood, but you might as well be. The both of you love to tempt fate."

"I don't believe in fate. We create our own destinies." Kahllah patted the gun in her harness. "Do you think you guys will be okay here while I go out for a few hours?"

Gucci shut the water off in the sink and gave Kahllah her full attention. "Yes, why wouldn't we be? Kahllah, the way you keep hovering like you're expecting something to happen is starting to make me nervous. Is there something you aren't telling me?"

"I don't mean to scare you, Gucci. It's just that this situation doesn't feel right to me. There are too many unknowns for my tastes. I just want to make sure that my loved ones are safe. Sorry if I'm being a mother-hen about it."

"No need to apologize, I'm used to it by now. Animal is the same way when he's home. You know, he's been removed from the streets for years, but he still carries himself like he's at war, constantly checking the house to make sure it's secure. And don't get me started on all the damn guns he keeps stashed around the house. I made him stash most of them in the garage, but he still insists on making sure there are at least three in the house at all times," she grabbed a box of cereal from the cabinet and removed a small .22 from it. "Who the hell stashes guns in the Captain Crunch?"

"A man who knows that life can go from sugar to shit in the blink of an eye," Kahllah said seriously. "I at least hope you're a better shot than you were when we first met. Remember that?"

Kahllah and Gucci's first meeting had been a rocky one. After Priest had rescued them from certain death, he tucked them away in an old church and appointed Kahllah their guard dog. She was supposed to keep them safe and attend to their needs, but she seemed more interested in testing Gucci. Kahllah blamed Gucci for Animal's beef with Shai Clark and it all came to a head one night.

Gucci and Kahllah were having a heated argument because Kahllah was questioning her dedication to Animal. Gucci had been riding with and for Animal for years and she was offended that his wayward sister had the nerve to call her character into question. She professed over and over that she would do anything for Animal, and Kahllah put her to the test.

"You say you love my brother, but how far are you willing to go to prove it?" Kahllah was asking.

"I'm willing to do whatever it takes," Gucci said confidently.

"It's easy to say it when it's just the two of us having girl talk, but what happens when you have to prove it? What do you do when his enemies are scratching at the door, and the only choices are to kill or be killed?"

"I do whatever it takes," Gucci said.

Kahllah regarded her for a few moments. She stood up and removed the gun from the holster clasped to the back of her pants and cocked the slide. Gucci watched nervously as Kahllah handed her the gun.

"What's this all about?" Gucci asked.

"Shoot me," Kahllah told her, shoving the gun into her hands.

"Kahllah, I ain't playing this sick little game with you," Gucci said.

"It ain't no game, Gucci. Shoot me," Kahllah repeated.

"Look, I'm not—"

"Gucci." Kahllah drew a blade from her bra and popped it open. "One of two things is going to happen. You're going to shoot me, or I'm going to cut your fucking throat."

Gucci studied Kahllah's face to see if she was serious. She was. When Gucci took too long to make up her mind, Kahllah moved in on her with the blade. Gucci raised the gun, finger hesitating on the trigger. She didn't want to kill Kahllah, but she didn't want to die, either. When it was clear to her that Kahllah intended on making good with her threat, Gucci pulled the trigger. Nothing happened.

Kahllah slapped Gucci's hand, sending the gun flying in the air. She fluidly moved behind Gucci and threw her into a chokehold, catching the gun with her free hand. She flicked the lever on the side of the pistol and dug the barrel into Gucci's cheek. "If I was one of Shai Clark's shooters, you'd be dead, all because you didn't know to take the safety off first," she whispered in Gucci's ear.

Gucci shoved Kahllah off her and spun in anger. "What the hell is your problem?"

"My problem is that you don't understand the seriousness of your situation. I don't know if you've been paying attention or not, but Animal isn't going to let this thing with Shai go, and that's your fault!"

"Animal is pressing the issue because he doesn't want to leave his friends in harm's way. You can't put this on me!"

"The hell I can't. My sucker-for-love-ass little brother came out of hiding because of *you*." She jabbed her finger at Gucci's chest. "He went at Shai Clark because of what happened to *you*." She jabbed her again. "And he's likely going to die because he loves *you*." Her voice was heavy with emotion. Although they had only met twice, she had been watching Animal for years and felt an attachment to him.

"You act like I asked for this to happen!" Gucci shouted. Kahllah's words cut her because of the truth in them. "I know I'm the cause of all this, but it's out of my hands. What am I supposed to do, Kahllah?"

Kahllah turned the gun, butt first, and shoved it into Gucci's chest, forcing her to take it. "When my brother's enemies come for him, be more than just a pretty fucking face."

"How could I forget, I thought your ass was certified crazy," Gucci chuckled, recalling the incident.

"Not crazy, just wanted you to be prepared," Kahllah said.

"After going through all this with Animal, I can now understand why. Your approach was suspect, but your message was received." Gucci expertly cocked the slide on the gun, chambering a round, before dumping the clip out and expelling the round into the air and catching it.

Kahllah smiled. "Very good, young Jedi. Glad Animal has taught you how to use it, but I hope you'll never have to."

"In this neighborhood? I doubt it. We're in the middle of the stix with nothing but old, rich white people around. I don't think we have too much to fear from them," Gucci joked. "But on another note, where are you off to today, all dolled up? You clean up pretty nice. You should try it more often," Gucci teased her.

"I'm going to follow up on a lead," Kahllah told her.

Gucci gave her the once over. "From where I'm standing this looks personal, not work related."

"Different prey calls for different bait," Kahllah told her. "I had a chit chat with an acquaintance and he suggested that my next clue in this mystery is in Watts."

Gucci didn't like it. "Kahllah, I don't know if it's a good idea for you to go over to that side of town by yourself, especially dressed like that. I know you're a bad ass assassin and all, but Watts is dangerous."

Kahllah opened her jacket, showing Gucci that she had two

guns in her harness as well as an assortment of blades. "So am I," she slid off the stool and headed for the door. On her way she stopped to kiss T.J. and Celeste on the tops of their heads. "You guys behave while I'm gone and Auntie K will bring you something back," he told them and left.

Gucci locked the door behind Kahllah, before leaning against it, closing her eyes and taking a deep breath. When she opened her eyes, she found Celeste watching, as she always was. Gucci sighed. "This is going to be a long day."

# PART III

## An Eye For An Eye

# SIXTEEN

"Everything good?" Animal asked Sonja in a concerned tone. They were riding in the back of a silver Denali on their way to the venue where George would be, so they could attempt the snatch grab.

After the fight between Ashanti and Cain at the house, they all figured it be best to take it down for the night and resume the next day. They needed to be well rested and fresh for the mission. Sonja and Animal checked into the hotel she had rented under a bogus name, while Ashanti opted to spend the night with Cain and Abel. To Animal's surprise, when they got to the hotel the front desk informed them that they'd only booked one room. Sonja claimed it was a mistake with the reservation, but Animal didn't believe her. They tried to rent an additional room, but the hotel was all booked up for the night, so Animal had no choice but to share a room with Sonja. He had totally prepared himself to spend the night fending off her sexual advances, but Sonja ended up going right to sleep. She was exhausted. Animal was tired too, but he couldn't sleep, he had too much on his mind. He sat up all night, flipping through the channels and chain smoking cigarettes. By the time he did get it in his mind to lay down for a while, it was already the next day and they had to make moves.

Before meeting back up with Ashanti and the twins, they stopped at a clothing store. Animal didn't understand her need to shop with all they had going on, but she explained that the shopping trip wasn't for her, it was for them. The club they would be invading had a strict dress code and they'd stick out wearing sneakers and jeans, so they needed outfits that would be deemed club appropriate. Animal didn't have a problem wearing the clothes that Sonja had picked out, but Ashanti and Abel threw fits. They were streets niggas and didn't take kindly to having to wear *"Monkey suits,"* as Abel had called them. It took some doing, but they finally relented and put on the clothes. Animal wore a simple white shirt and black jeans, cuffed over soft leather black shoes. Ashanti grabbed a sweater from the pile, and blue jeans, which left Abel with the last outfit by default. They laughed their asses off when he came out of the bathroom dressed in a cream colored suit that was a size too big. He looked funny as hell in the get up, but it would have to do because they didn't have time to find him something else.

After changing and arming themselves, they went to pick up the rental truck. One of Abel's jump-offs had rented it with her credit card for him. He wasn't worried about being connected to the rental truck, because the girl didn't know his real name, nor did she know where he lived. She was just a random chick he'd met one day, who he exchanged cash for ass with. Abel had a plethora of simple-minded young girls who were willing to do whatever he asked in exchange for some attention or a few dollars.

Cain drove with Abel riding shotgun. Animal and Red Sonja occupied the second row, while Ashanti was in the back, checking over all the guns to make sure they were loaded and functional. They'd been passing around blunts, and going over last minute details of the plan when Sonja got the phone call that completely shifted the energy in the truck.

"I just received word that three of the men who helped me escape the island were executed as traitors," Sonja continued. "She dumped their headless bodies in the town square to rot and forbid anyone to remove them until the crows have had their fill."

"That's one hell of a way to send a message," Cain said from behind the wheel.

"She wanted to make sure I heard it . . . and I did." Sonja was saddened by the news of the multiple executions. She didn't know the men well who had helped her, but they had always been loyal to her father's army, and her as their general.

"Do the men know where you were headed?" Animal asked. She didn't have to respond, the look on her face said it all. "Damn," Animal cursed. If Sonja's position was compromised, so was the entire mission. This changed everything.

"We can do it another time. It's too risky to try tonight without being sure what Lilith's people know or don't know," Sonja said. She already had three deaths on her hands and couldn't hold four more.

"And wait until next month when he makes another trip

to try it all over again? Nah, we're doing this tonight," Animal insisted.

"Big homie, you sure?" Ashanti asked.

"Not really, but time to wait is a luxury I don't have. I ain't asking you to put your nuts on the table with me on this."

"That's because you don't have to ask. Some things go without saying. You ride, I ride, straight like that," Ashanti said.

"And what about you?" Animal addressed Abel, who was sitting in the passenger seat next to his brother. Animal knew what Ashanti was capable of, so it was never really a question, but this was his first time riding out with Abel. He watched the young man's face, looking for signs of uncertainty.

Abel looked back at Animal, eyes low and red from the weed they'd been passing around. "Well, if I'm bound for the casket, at least I'm already dressed for the occasion," he tugged at the lapels of the suit jacket he was wearing. "We do this three the hard way.""I don't like it," Cain said, expressing his displeasure. The plan had stunk from the time they cracked the package, and the smell became more ripe the longer it sat out.

"It ain't about what you like, it's about what needs to be done. You wanna take a powder and wash your hands with it, nobody is gonna hold it against you," Ashanti assured him.

"Just because it's a dumb ass plan doesn't mean I'm gonna leave y'all hanging. I'm in," Cain said.

Cain and Sonja dropped the three desperados off two doors down from the club entrance. There was a small alleyway between two of the buildings that would lead them around to the back of the nightclub. Sonja's friend would be waiting for them at the service entrance.

"Everybody locked and loaded?" Animal asked, stepping out of the truck. He took a second to make sure the palm-sized Glock he was carrying had one in the chamber.

"You know it," Ashanti said, slipping a .32 into his pants pocket.

"If that's what you wanna call it," Abel looked at his .22, frowning. "If shit gets thick, what kinda damage are these pop shooters gonna do?"

"They're easier to conceal than a machine gun," Animal told him. The success of their mission would depend on speed and stealth. They had to attract as little attention as possible and didn't want to have unnatural looking bulges putting them on security's radar. "With any luck you won't need the hardware. Your job is to make sure we got a clear path outta there when this goes down. We'll be moving fast and don't need anything or anyone in the way."

"What if it's a civilian that gets in the way?" Abel asked.

"Ain't no civilians tonight. Anybody tries to play hero, you put a hole in them and keep moving. Us getting out alive trumps everything else."

"I think I can handle that," Abel said.

"Hopefully we can pull this off without having to use these hammers. Gunshots bring police," Animal said.

"Homie, ain't no way we gonna go in there and snatch this dude without having to use these pistols. Not unless you know a magic trick," Ashanti said.

"He does," Sonja gave him a wink. "Animal will fill you in once you guys are inside. Now get moving, and be careful," she said, almost like an order. The general was coming out of her. Sonja watched as the three men disappeared into the alley, praying their backs wouldn't be the last images she had of them. Sonja got out of the back seat, and jumped in front next to Cain. "Circle the block a few times, and be ready to snatch our boys when they come out of there."

Animal and the others stayed close to the wall, as they parted the two buildings. Animal peeked around the corner to make sure the coast was clear before continuing. They darted from shadow to shadow until they reached the back of the club where Ashanti and Abel crouched behind a dumpster while Animal approached the door. He rapped on it in the specified pattern and waited. It was only a few seconds, but it felt like an hour before someone opened the back door.

He was an older black dude, wearing a stained white cook's shirt and plaid pants. The center of his head was balding, and the sides were sprinkled with the same scruffy grey hair that lined his chin. When his weary eyes landed on Animal, he squinted suspiciously.

"Got a few strays that need feeding. Think you can spare a few scraps?" Animal asked.

The older man acknowledged it was the right code phrase and let them in. "You got something for me?" he asked Animal as Ashanti and Abel crept inside.

Animal pulled an envelope from his pocket and handed it to the old man. He didn't bother to count it. He just stuffed it inside his white shirt. "Go through those doors, and pass the bathroom and it'll put you in the main area. The man you're looking for has a booth upstairs on the second level.

He's got three bodyguards with him that I counted," he gave Animal a quick run down. "You're on your own from here, and if anything goes wrong I don't know you or Sonja, ya dig?" Without waiting for an answer he slunk back into the kitchen.

Ashanti stood beside Animal. "So far so good, huh?"

"So far," Animal looked towards the doors the old man had directed them to and felt his stomach shift a bit. Past that point, there would be no turning back.

"So you got any idea how we're supposed to get this guy out without having to kill a bunch of people?" Abel asked Animal.

"We'll walk him out," Animal opened his hand and revealed two small syringes.

"What the hell is that?" Ashanti asked, carefully plucking one of the syringes from Animal's hand. He turned it end over end, studying the piss colored liquid inside.

"A sedative, courtesy of Red Sonja. If we can get him alone we'll pump him full of this. It won't knock him out, but it'll disorient him enough to where we can stroll out of here with him like we're just trying to help our drunk friend home," Animal explained.

Abel nodded. "That's some slick shit on your part."

"It was Sonja's idea," Animal admitted.

"That Red Sonja is just full of ideas. For this to have happened so suddenly, it seems like Red Sonja has had quite a bit of time to think through the details, doesn't it?" Ashanti asked suspiciously.

"Sonja is military, so I expect her to be thorough, even on short notice," Animal told him.

"If you say so, big homie." Ashanti let it go. He picked up

on the uncertainty in Animal's voice, but didn't want to say anything in front of Abel to create doubt. Animal was leading them, and Ashanti needed everyone to be as confident in Animal's leadership skills as he was. Still, he would keep a close eye on Red Sonja until this was all over.

# SEVENTEEN

THE PLACE THAT KAHLLAH WAS LOOKING for didn't prove too hard to find. It was located in a less than savory part of town. It was one of the smaller establishments on the block, a storefront to be exact. Above the doorway flew a flag sporting two stars, one red and one blue. For a social club, it didn't look very social.

Kahllah took a few minutes to make sure her guns were loaded and her blades were accessible. She had done some digging into Panama Black to get a better idea of what she was up against and couldn't find more then a few random articles that mentioned his name. He was like a ghost in all the city and state databases, and she dared not try to check him against the federal records. If the Brotherhood was watching her, which they likely were, they'd know the minute she used her pass code to accessed the files and it would tip them off that she was getting closer to the truth. She had to keep her investigation off the grid for as long as she could.

As Kahllah strolled towards the entrance of the bar, she spotted two older men sitting on crates and playing chess on a piece of cardboard. Even though she felt like she was dressed like the Happy-Hooker, the old men were so into their game they never so much as gave her a second look. Just as Kahllah was walking into the place, one of the waitresses was coming out, carrying two sodas. They collided in the doorway, causing the soda to splash on Kahllah's jacket.

She was a pretty young Spanish girl, who appeared to be in her early twenties. The uniform skirt and wore, hugged her thick thighs so tight that it was a wonder she could walk in it.

"Sorry about that, I didn't see you coming," Kahllah apologized. "Let me pay for the sodas," she offered.

"No, no, it was my fault," the girl said nervously. Don't trouble yourself," she said and hurried off to give the chess players what was left of the soda.

From the girl's speedy departure, she had no doubt felt the harness under Kahllah's jacket when they collided. The question now was, would Kahllah be able to get in and out with the information she needed before the girl tipped someone off? She had to move quick.

It took a few seconds for Kahllah's eyes to adjust to the poor lighting. The place looked even smaller on the inside as it did the outside. There was only enough room for a small horseshoe bar, a pool table and a few tables and chairs. Normally she would've cased the joint a few days before the job, but this was short notice. The smell of sweat and smoke in the cramped room was so offensive that she had to breathe through her mouth.

The few men who had been sitting on the bar stool immediately turned their attention to Kahllah. Most of them were Panamanian, or of other Hispanic descent, and they all wore hard faces. She could feel them watching her as she crossed

the room. Predatory stares and visions of her naked, dancing behind drunken eyes. It was all she could do to keep from
breaking the hand of a man who had tried to grab her ass when
she passed him.

Kahllah took a seat at the end of the bar, closest to the bathroom. It gave her the best view of the entire place. The waitress
she'd collided with came back inside. When she saw Kahllah sitting at the bar, she did everything in her power to avoid making
eye contact with her. Kahllah watched the waitress, as she went
to a table full of tough looking men in the back to take their drink
orders. She saw one of them, presumably their leader, grab a fist
full of her bottom. The girl made no attempt to move his hand
so Kahllah figured it was part of whatever arrangement the girl
had with the regulars who frequented the place. The girl spared a
glance behind her at Kahllah, but didn't let her eyes linger.

It only took a few seconds for the bartender to approach
her, sitting a shot glass and a beer in front of her. He was a sour
looking old man, wearing a dirty tank top under a leather vest.

"I didn't order anything," Kahllah told him.

"I know, those are on the house," he said with a thick accent.
"We welcome all new and pretty faces to our establishment this
way."

"That's sad, because I was starting to feel like I was special,"
Kahllah faked disappointment.

"Oh, you're special indeed. Hands down the prettiest woman
I've ever seen come through these doors," the bartender poured
it on thick. "Sweetheart, your money is no good here. Anything
you need, you come to me."

"Funny you should offer, because I'm in need of something . . . information," Kahllah told him.

The bartender frowned. "You want information, I suggest you dial four-one-one."

"Already tried that, and the information I need isn't listed. You seem like an important man about the world and I was thinking maybe you could help me out," Kahllah placed something under a napkin and slid it across the bar to the bartender. His greedy eyes lit up when he saw the folded hundred dollar bills.

The bartender gave a cautious look around before sliding the money into his pocket. "We might be able to help each other out after all. What do you need to know?" "I need to know how to find Panama Black."

At the mention of the gangster's name, the bartender's face drained of all its color. He took the money out of his pocket and slid it back to Kahllah. "I'm sorry, afraid I can't help you," when he tried to remove his hand, Kahllah grabbed his wrist and held his hand flat on the bar.

"From the load you probably just took in your pants, I take it you know Panama Black well enough to be afraid of him," Kahllah observed.

The bartender leaned in and whispered to Kahllah. "Listen, little girl, I don't know what your game is, but you need to be mindful of the stakes you're playing for. You do not want to find Panama Black."

The waitress came to the bar to grab two waiting beers for her table. She took one look at the exchange going on between Kahllah and the bartender, and hurried away with the beers. She knew the moment she saw Kahllah walk in that she was trouble and wanted no part of it.

"But indeed I do," Kahllah assured him. "I'm willing to pay

for the information," she produced a small blade from some-where inside her jacket and placed it over the bartender's pinky finger, "or get to cutting pieces off you until you feel like shar-ing. It's your call." While Kahllah was waiting for the bartender to make his choice, her eyes drifted to the mirror behind the bar. She saw the men who had been sitting at the table in the back exchange words with the waitress, before getting up and heading in her direction. She could only imagine what the girl had told them, but she didn't have to guess at what they were coming to do.

The leader of their group, the man Kahllah had seen palm the girl's ass, led the group with a purposeful stride. He was a muscular man, wearing a white t-shirt and a bandana on his head that was a replica of the Panamanian flag. As soon as she saw him raise his hand to touch her, she went into action.

Kahllah spun on the barstool, grabbed the leader by the arm, and stabbed him twice in the belly with the blade she'd been threatening the bartender with. His body had barely hit the ground before she sent the blade flaying, stabbing the man closest to him in the throat. Seeing her kill two men in two sec-onds gave the rest of the men food for thought, and sent them running.

Kahllah turned her attention back to the bartender just in time to see him pulling the slide on the shotgun that had been hidden under the bar. She ducked just as the powerful spray of buckshots sailed over her head. A few stray pellets peppered her neck and shoulder. They didn't do any major damage, but the fragments hurt like hell. She wished she'd had the good sense to wear her body armor, but there was no way she would've been able to hide it under the tight jacket.

Before the bartender could get off another round, Kahllah had bounded to the bar and was smashing the heel of her bootie into his chest. The bartender fell into the rack of glasses and bottles behind him, bringing the whole thing crashing to the ground. He tried to get to his feet, but a kick from Kahllah to the ribs sent him back down. She dragged him up by his hair and slammed his head against the bar twice, before laying his neck on the bar top like a chopping block. From the spine of her harness, she drew a nasty looking short sword and laid the edge of the blade against the bartender's throat.

"You're the third muthafucka in almost as many days who didn't know how to answer a simple fucking question without taking a swing at me or trying to have me killed. One of them is dead and one of them wishes that he was dead. Which side of that coin are you going to fall on?" Kahllah asked him.

"Okay, okay . . . I know Panama Black," the bartender admitted.

"That's obvious to a fucking duck. Now where can I find him?"

"I don't know. I haven't seen him around in a few days," the bartender told her.

Kahllah raised the sword, poised to take his head. "Why don't I believe you?"

"I swear to God, I'm telling you the truth. Panama used to come in here all the time, but a few days ago he went missing. Nobody has seen him," the bartender said honestly.

"What about his girlfriend? They say she works in this place. Where can I find her?"

"That's the same thing I want to know," a voice called from the door. Kahllah spun, drawing one of her guns with her free hand, ready to gun down the new threat. To her relief, it was just one of the old men who had been sitting outside playing chess. "That girl was supposed to replace the soda she spilled, but she never came back."

Realization hit Kahllah like a slap in the face. The Spanish girl! She'd no doubt overheard Kahllah asking about Panama Black, and used the thugs in the bar as a distraction while she slipped out, no doubt to warn Panama Black. Kahllah had officially lost the element of surprise. Had she not been so deadset on revenge, she would've made sure she knew what Panama's girlfriend looked like before she came to the bar. Once again she had let her emotions get in the way of her mission. There was nothing she could do about it now, except follow through. She just hoped that Animal and Red Sonja were having better luck than she was dealing with their problem.

# EIGHTEEN

IT HAD BEEN A LONG TIME SINCE Animal had been inside a club. If he recalled correctly, the last time he had been in one was to do harm to someone, much like that night. As soon as they hit the main floor they split up, with Ashanti mixing in with the crowd, and Abel positioning himself near the hallway where they had come in. Animal pushed a path through the crowd to the bar and leaned with his back to it.

From where Animal was standing, he had a clear view of the second floor, where George was. The VIP area was not as crowded as the main level, but there were enough people to where it took Animal a few minutes to pick George out. George wore a plain white t-shirt, with blue jeans and heavy jewelry. Animal could tell just by the way the light was catching the diamonds in his chain that it had cost a few dollars. He was sitting on the back-rest of one of the booths, drinking champagne from the bottle. There were several females at his booth, fawning over him like he was God's gift, while he smiled and talked shit amongst them. George looked more like a rapper than a kingpin's step-kid.

The old man had said George had three guards with him, but Animal could only spot two. They sat on opposite sides of George like bookends. They were both mean looking Hispanic dudes, one with a mustache and the other clean-shaven. Their keen eyes watched everyone who ventured too close to George, ready to go into action at a moment's notice. Not even the females vying for the group's attention could distract them. They were no amateurs, all business and likely to be Animal's biggest obstacles, next to actually gaining entrance to the VIP. Security at the bottom of the stairs was checking everybody for the proper colored wristbands and those who didn't have them were getting turned away. He needed to find a way to get up there.

"Sweetie, if you're not ordering a drink I'm going to need you to clear the bar," a feminine voice said behind Animal. He turned and found himself looking at the bartender. She was a statuesque dark skinned dime, with a head full of expensive weave and a pretty smile. When she saw Animal's face a light of recognition went off in here head. "Is that little Animal?"

Animal was taken back. The girl looked familiar, but he didn't think he knew her. "I think you've got me confused with someone else."

"Knock it off, I'd know you anywhere. You used to live on my block in Brooklyn," she told him, but Animal still didn't make the connection. The girl sighed. "I know it's been a long time, but I couldn't have changed that much. I'm Lizzy, Kastro's home girl."

When she dropped Kastro's name the pieces fell into place. Lizzy was one of the girls who used to hang around the apartment building where Animal was staying. The people in the neighborhood had affectionately nicknamed it Hell, because it was an unsavory place where you could satisfy all your vices. Hell was open to any and all misfits who needed a place to stay and were willing to work to earn their keep. Back then Lizzy was just a little girl who used to hang around running errands for Kastro, but she was all grown up now. The last time he'd seen her it had been his sixteenth birthday and she delivered him a gift from Kastro that would change his life.

The day of his sixteenth birthday, Tech had gotten all of the gang together and threw Animal a birthday barbecue on the block. Animal remembered it clearly because it was the first time he'd seen Ashanti after being missing for a couple of years. They were catching up on old times when a late model Honda with tinted windows pulled up to the curb. It was an unfamiliar car, so everyone was instantly on point, ready to pop off at a moment's notice. Surprisingly, a cute dark-skinned girl got out on the passenger's side and stepped onto the curb. It was Lizzy. She was carrying a large gift bag in her hand and looking over Animal's rag-tag crew like they were something vile. "Anybody know where I can find Animal?"

Silk, who was new to the crew at the time, stepped up. "Nah, but I'm Silk if you're looking for a good time."

Lizzy rolled her eyes at Silk. "Sweetie, I'm strictly dickly, and I have a man. I just came to drop something off for Animal from a friend, so either you know where he is or you don't."

"I'm Animal." He stepped forward. As he got closer to Lizzy, he realized he had seen her before. She was one of Kastro's errand girls and the one who had told them about the death of Tango.

Lizzy smiled and held out the bag. "This is from Kastro. She says to tell you 'Happy Birthday.'"

At the mention of Kastro's name, Animal's face lit up. Kastro and a bunch of the others had been arrested a few months prior when the police raided her apartment and killed her brother, Gladiator. Animal hadn't seen or heard from her since she'd been locked up.

"How's she doing?" he asked as he accepted the bag.

"She's doing good, but she's been better. She's still locked up, fighting the case from the raid, but things are looking good for her," Lizzy informed him.

"I'm glad to hear it. I was worried about her," Animal said.

"No need to be. You know Kastro is a survivor," Lizzy replied.

"So what is it?" Animal hoisted the bag.

"I have no idea. She just said to make sure that I gave it to you and to tell you to open the gift when you're somewhere private. I've done my part, so I'm gone," Lizzy started back to the car, but Animal called after her.

"Thank you, and tell Kastro that I love her," Animal said.

Lizzy smiled. "I will. And happy birthday, Animal," she told him before getting back into her car and pulling off.

After Lizzy had gone, Animal, Tech and Ashanti went up to Tech's apartment to open the gift and see what it was. Animal's hands trembled nervously as he tore off the wrapping paper. It was a wooden box with a gold clasp and the words, *"For my favorite misfit."* were engraved into the top. When Animal opened the box and saw what was inside, his heart was aflutter. They were two Glocks with rose-tinted barrels and rubber grips. It was the first time he had ever held his Pretty Bitches and he fell instantly in love with the custom guns.

"It's been a long time," Animal said.

"Too long," Lizzy agreed. "Last I heard, you were doing like a hundred years in prison."

"Don't go believing everything you hear, ma. I had a spot of legal trouble, but it's all behind me now," Animal said.

"Well, I'm glad the rumors weren't true. Oh, and I'm sorry to hear about Kastro. It broke my heart when I heard she got killed," Lizzy said sincerely.

"Mine too," Animal said, remembering Kastro's murder. She had been trying o help him rescue Gucci when Shai's men got the drop on her. Kastro was a gangster to the end, cutting Angelo's face before he blew her brains out. Animal took her death extremely hard. Kastro was yet another person who had been hurt because of him, and he vowed one day to settle up for her life. Truce or not, Angelo would answer for killing his friend.

"Sorry, I didn't men to be all depressing," Lizzy said, noticing the change on Animal's face.

"It's okay. So, what've you been up to all these years?" Animal changed the subject.

"Working and trying to raise my kids," Lizzy told him.

"Oh, you got kids now? Congratulations."

"Yeah, a boy and a girl," Lizzy pointed to the tattoo of the two young faces on her forearm. "They're my hearts."

"I know what you mean. I have two myself," Animal said, thinking of T.J., Celeste and the reason he was there that night.

"Well, I know things are busy in here tonight and I don't wanna keep you. It was good seeing you, Lizzy," he attempted to leave, but she stopped him.

"Wait a minute, Animal. It's rare that I get to see anybody from the old neighborhood since I moved to the Bronx. Before you rush off, at least have a drink with me," Lizzy said.

Lizzy offered without offering. He had to admit that she had filled out quite nicely, but he had a wife and a mission to complete. "Lizzy, I'd love to, but I don't know if I'll still be around when your shift is over. I just stopped through for a minute then I'm getting out of here," he was trying to give her a gentle brush off, but Lizzy was persistent.

"We don't have to wait until my shift is over. I can't drink here on the main floor, but in about fifteen minutes, I'm switching with the bartender in the VIP. They don't much care what we do up there, as long as the register doesn't come up short."

At the mention of the VIP, Animal had an idea. Lizzy might prove to be helpful after all. "Sounds like a plan."

After Lizzy's relief arrived, she lead Animal to the staircase that went up to the VIP. On the way Animal passed Ashanti, who was giving him a questioning look. Animal motioned to him to wait, and kept walking with Lizzy. The bouncer at the bottom of the stairs looked like he was going to give them trouble, but he stepped aside and let them up when he found out he was with Lizzy. He mumbled something slick under his breath, but didn't try to stop Animal from going up.

If what was going on in the main area could've been considered a good time, then the VIP was a blast. Liquor was flowing, blunts were being passed and there was not a sober soul in the bunch. It was crowded with mostly females, and the few men who had the cake to foot the ticket. Lizzy had explained to Animal that to party upstairs was a five bottle minimum, and the cheapest bottle was five hundred dollars. Animal found this laughable. Even during his moment in the limelight, when he was signed to Big Dawg, Animal never wasted his money the way they did. It was insane to pay five times the normal cost of something just to look good in public.

Being upstairs, Animal was able to get a better scope of the layout. Immediately to his left sat George and his crew. Up close, he was smaller than Animal thought, almost to the point of being petite. Big stones glistened on nearly every finger of the hand he had wrapped around a bottle of champagne. He was laughing so hard at something someone had said that he spilled champagne on one of the girls closest to him. Her dress was ruined, but she didn't seem to mind. The two bodyguards Animal had spotted earlier were now standing at opposite ends of the booth, giving up their seats to the women entertaining George. Their faces were sour and their eyes were on high alert.

Animal followed Lizzy to the VIP bar, which was smaller than the one downstairs, but less crowded. There were a few people around the bar, waiting for Lizzy so they could fill their drink orders, but for the most part, the waitresses shuttled the drinks back and forth from the bar to patrons, so they didn't have to be bothered.

"Grab a seat and give me two minutes to get situated," Lizzy told Animal, before going behind the bar to take over.

Animal found an empty seat at the end of the bar that allowed him to watch George without having to look directly at him. If Animal had to describe George's personality he'd have said it was *big*. Animal found himself fascinated by the way people flocked to George. He seemed to have a magnetic personality that was usually reserved for entertainers, or politicians. A part of him wondered what George could've been in life if he'd been born to a different mother and not been a necessary evil in the grand scheme of Animal's life. Didn't much matter anymore what George could've been, all that remained is what he was . . . leverage.

Animal paid special attention to George's two bodyguards. From the distasteful glances they cast at him every time he gave an order, he deduced they didn't care for him very much. From the set of their posture, Animal could tell that the two men were more soldiers than babysitters. Everybody in their group had a drink in their hands or a blunt in their mouths, except the two bodyguards. Occasionally they'd sip from glasses of ice water, but they didn't touch anything that would impair them. Animal knew the biggest part of his problem would be getting them off point. Dosing George with the sedative and getting him past the guard dogs was clearly out of the question, but it was all Animal had at the moment. His daughter's life depended on George's abduction, so most of Sonja's well-laid plan would have to be improvised on the fly. If he could just get enough separation between them and George, he had a fighter's chance.

While observing George, another player came into the game . . . the third bodyguard. Animal knew this because the other two bodyguards barely gave him a second look when he came over to present several more girls for George to choose from. He exchanged a few words with George, before offering the ladies seats and helping himself to a glass of vodka. The other two bodyguards gave the third distasteful looks, as he sipped hard liquor and partied with George. Animal had found the weakest link in the chain.

"Here you go," Lizzy got his attention when she placed a glass on the bar in front of him.

Animal looked at the brown liquid suspiciously.

"It's Hennessy, not poison," Lizzy smiled. "I'm not sure if you still fuck with it, but I remember how much you liked it when we were younger. I used to hear Kastro all the way on the stoop cursing y'all out about going in her Henny stash."

"It was good then and it's still good now," Animal almost downed the liquor. The burning quickly spread through his limbs, and made him feel more relaxed. He probably shouldn't have had the drink, considering he was technically on the clock, but he didn't want to offend Lizzy, especially since he still might need her before the night was over. The one shout wasn't enough to get him drunk, but the second one she placed down in front of him would no doubt open up the possibility.

Animal took his time with the second shot, nursing it, listening to Lizzy talk about her life, faking interest. While she blabbed on, he watched George and his men. The third bodyguard was far looser than the first, pouring liquor down the thirsty throats of women and having a good time. George didn't seem bothered by him neglecting his responsibilities, but it didn't sit well with the other two bodyguards. They exchanged dirty looks every time the third one touched a bottle or hit a blunt. One of them even tried to say something to him about it, but he waved him off. The other bodyguard reached for his bottle of water and realized it was empty. Animal saw him motion to the empty bottle and say something to the third bodyguard, no doubt sending him for a refill. The third bodyguard said something back that didn't look pleasant, but when George intervened, he wisely closed his mouth and went to do as he was told. When Animal saw him coming towards the bar, the wheels of his mind started spinning.

"It's hot as hell in here," the third bodyguard said to no one in particular when he reached the bar. He was sweating like a runaway slave, partially due to the heat and partially due to the liquor he was rapidly consuming.

"Yeah, hot as a sauna," Animal engaged him in conversation. He could tell he was the chatty type, so he cut right into him. "The only good thing about this heat is it's making the ladies come out of their clothes," he nodded to a girl who was on a nearby table, dancing on it wearing nothing but her bra.

The third guard watched her for a few seconds. "She's nice, but we've got all the best ones with us."

"I noticed," Animal glanced over his shoulder at their booth like a star-struck groupie. "If you guys find yourselves with more women than you can handle, I'll be happy to take a few off your hands."

"Sorry, my man. Those are for members only, but you're welcome to whatever stragglers my boss doesn't pick to leave with us tonight," he patted Animal on his back a little too hard for his taste. The man was obviously wasted or well on his way. "Yo shorty," he called to Lizzy, who was behind the bar taking another drink order, "let me get another bottle of Goose."

Lizzy held up one finger for him to give her a second, while she took care of the people ahead of him and he didn't seem to appreciate getting put off.

"Come on with that finger shit, we spending too much money in here to be kept waiting," the third bodyguard capped.

"Put all that shit on my man's tab." He didn't have to be so rude, but he was trying to impress Animal or anyone else who might've been listening. "I swear man, you give these bitches a little position and they get besides themselves."

"I know how it goes, bro. Chicks ain't dependable for shit except a quick nut," Animal fed into it.

"Or a long nut," the third bodyguard gave Animal dap. He wasn't sure what it was, but there was something about the wild haired young dude with the gold teeth that he liked.

Lizzy came back over to that side of the bar and slammed a bottle of Grey Goose on the bar, giving the third bodyguard a dirty look.

"Where my waters at? C'mon, if you gonna do ya job, don't do it half ass," the third bodyguard said to Lizzy. "And while you at it; pour two more shots of whatever my man right here is drinking."

Lizzy opened her mouth to say something, but thought better of it. She knew the man's group had been in the club spending thousands and if she offended him she could very well loose her job. Painfully biting her tongue, she went off to get the shots and the waters.

"I appreciate that, but you don't have to. I ain't broke," Animal told him.

"Chill out, kid. Nobody is trying to call you broke, I dig your style and wanted to treat you to a drink, that's all," the third bodyguard told him.

Lizzy came back and placed the bottles of water and two shots on the bar top, along with a bill and walked away.

The third bodyguard picked up the bill and balled it up. "You see what I mean about doing a half ass job?" he tossed the crumbled slip of paper behind the bar. "I told her to put it on my man's tab, but she acting like she don't hear me. Dumb ass broad. But fuck all that, let's have a quick toast so I can get back. To my man . . . . say, what's your name kid?"

"Tech," Animal lied. It was the first name that popped into his head.

The third bodyguard let the name roll around in his head. "With a name like Tech, you must be about that life."

Animal shrugged. "I know how to handle myself pretty good in a tight situation."

"I hear you talking. To my man, Tech," he hoisted the shot glass. Animal and the third bodyguard touched glasses and they both threw back the shots. "It was good meeting you, Tech," he extended his hand.

"Good meeting you too, fam." When Animal went to shake the third bodyguard's hand, he purposely knocked over a discarded beer bottle, spilling what was left of the beer on the third bodyguard's outfit. "Damn, my bad."

"You clumsy little muthafucka," the third bodyguard jumped back, trying to wipe the beer from his clothes with his hands.

The third bodyguard called Animal everything but a child of God, while trying to clean himself up. He was more concerned about his expensive shirt than the drinks, and for a few seconds he took his eyes off the bottle. That was all the time Animal needed. He slipped the remaining syringe from his pocket quickly jammed it through each water bottle top, ejecting the liquid.

"Nigga, you just ruined a five hundred dollar shirt," the third bodyguard continued.

"I'm really sorry. Let me pay for it," Animal offered. He reached in his pocket and the third bodyguard took a cautious step back, fearing Animal would spill something else on him.

"I don't want nothing from your clumsy ass but to stay away from me," the third bodyguard snatched the Grey Goose and both water bottles from the bar. "And to think I was about to invite your clown ass over to our section," he shook his head and walked away.

Animal watched at the third bodyguard went back over to his group, and animatedly tried to explain why he had come back wet. The third bodyguard continued with his war story, placing the Grey Goose on the table and giving the waters to his comrades. From the way everyone was laughing and looking in Animal's direction, the third bodyguard had no doubt spun the tale to where Animal ended up looking like a clown, but it didn't matter. The incident had served its purpose. After seeing how tight George's security was, Animal knew drugging him and getting him out would've been near impossible, so he came up with the alternative plan of drugging his security. Being that he had to split the sedative between the two of them he had no idea how affective it would be, but all he needed was a window of opportunity. If they slipped, even for a second, he could take them . . . or so he hoped.

Animal walked over to the short glass wall that overlooked the main area, and leaned on his elbows, scanning the crowd. Abel was right where he was supposed to be, making sure they had a clear path out. He found Ashanti on the other side, stalking to a girl. Ashanti must've felt that he was being watched, because he suddenly looked up. Animal flashed ten fingers, letting him know it was going down in ten minutes.

Ashanti nodded, and excused himself from the girl to take his position.

Now that the pieces were in place, Animal needed to set the tumblers in motion. He pulled out his cell phone and hit a button, then waited and watched. The sour bodyguard had just opened one of the bottles of water and taken a big gulp, when the caller on the other end of Animal's phone picked up. "In about ten minutes I need a distraction, but it's gonna have to be a big one."

"You sure about this?" Cain asked, looking at Red Sonja like she was crazy.

"He says he needs a distraction. What's a better distraction than a stampede?" Sonja pulled a Mac 11 from the floor of the backseat.

Cain turned down the block of the club, where they had dropped Animal and the others off, and slowed the car down as they passed. Red Sonja leaned out the window, eyes locked on the crowd of people standing on the line waiting to get in. One of the bystanders spotted Sonja hanging out the window with the gun, and moved to alert the club security, but it was already too late.

The loud retort of the Mac 11 woke up the whole block. Sonja swept the gun across the front of the club, shattering windows and sending people scattering. She was careful not to hit any of the civilians standing outside, but couldn't speak for anybody unfortunate enough to be standing on the other side of the glass. When they'd originally set out, they agreed to keep casualties to a minimum, but Sonja needed to get off. She was a ball of anger and the rattling of the gun in her hands was the only thing that seemed to soothe her. By the time Sonja was done, several dead bodies littered the sidewalk and the club was thrown into total chaos.

"Damn, now that's how you create a fucking diversion!" Cain said excitedly. He was so animated that the Denali swerved and nearly sideswiped a parked car.

"Calm your ass down and pay attention to the road," Sonja barked. "Spin back around the block. They should be coming out with George any second now."

Watching Red Sonja sitting there, holding a smoking machine gun, made Cain smile inwardly. Up until then he hadn't cared for her much, but now he was on the fence. She was just as nuts as he was and it kind of turned him on.

# NINETEEN

Animal leaned against the railing, watching and wait-ing. The night was winding down and George looked nice and faded. He would likely be making his exit soon. It took a while for the affects of the sedatives to kick in, but they did . . . at least with one of the bodyguards. The smaller of the two had gone from standing at his post to sitting on the arm of the chair. Every few seconds he would wipe the sweat from his face with a napkin. The sour bodyguard was still on his feet. Outside of the fact that he was now leaning against the wall instead of stand-ing upright were the only signs that the sedative had even hit him at all. Whether it had hit him or not, Animal would have to make his move.

His cell phone vibrated, drawing his attention away from George and his group. He looked down at the screen and saw *Sis* flash across the screen. It was Kahllah's fifth time calling, no doubt to check on their progress. Animal had been preoccu-pied with his scheming the last few times she called, so she was probably getting nervous. He figured he'd better pick up just to tell her that things were okay before she ended up hopping a flight to New York. He was just about to answer the phone, when he heard the sound of glass breaking, followed by the unmistakable tatter of gunfire. Kahllah would have to wait. It was game time.

The whole club was thrown into a panic. People were trampling each other trying to get to the exits. Animal saw Abel press himself against the wall, and draw his gun. He looked confused and agitated, and for a minute Animal thought he would bolt with the rest of the crowd, but Abel held his position, and guarded their exit. Ashanti was right, he was a good soldier.

Animal could also see Ashanti moving in and out of the crowd, getting closer to the stairs that led to the VIP. The bouncer had his back to Ashanti, trying to help with crowd control. Ashanti rolled up behind him and clubbed him in the head with something, before vanishing again, swallowed by the crowd. Animal had lost sight of Ashanti, but he wasn't worried. He knew his friend would be there when and if he needed him. Now it was time snatch the prize.

Frightened partygoers and employees alike surged towards the steps, trying to get out of the VIP. Nobody knew where the shots were coming from and it didn't matter. When someone was shooting, you moved. It was a zoo, which was a good thing for Animal because it would make his job easier. He would be a needle in a haystack.

George's bodyguards were immediately on their feet with their guns drawn when they heard the shooting. The first bodyguard, the one with the sour face, moved on sluggishly, shoving a path through the crowd, while the other two flanked George.

They were trying to get him to the VIP stairs and out of the club. Animal held his gun at his side, sliding in and out of the crowd, stalking his prey and inching ever closer. He was so close to George that he could smell the fear coming off him.

Animal raised his gun, taking aim at the head of the body-guard who was bringing up the rear, the same loudmouth who had brought him a shot. Seeing him go down would shock them long enough for Animal to take out the other two body-guards then make off with George. His finger caressed the trigger, communicating to it what he needed done and the precise time to do it. At the same time he pulled the trigger, one of the fleeing partygoers stumbled into him and sent the shot wild.

All eyes were now on Animal, including those of George and his bodyguards. Animal let off another shot, but ended up hitting an innocent bystander who had accidentally stepped into his line of fire. The bodyguards returned fire, forcing Animal to scramble backward, firing back. Animal dove behind the bar just as a hail of bullets tore through it. He kept his head down, crawling into the furthest corner of the bar, while trying not to get shot. Animal's hand slipped in something wet, and he almost lost his balance. He looked at his hand and noticed that it was slick with blood. His eyes followed the trial of blood, and though he feared he knew what he would find, his mind still wasn't prepared for it. Laying on her side, just under where the register sat, was Lizzy. Her eyes stared at Animal, but did not see him. There was a gaping hole in her forehead, which was leaking blood and brain matter over her face and onto the floor. Another life had been taken because of him and two more kids would have to grow up without a parent. At that point there wasn't much Animal could do, besides make sure his kids didn't have to grow up the same way. He would mourn Lizzy after he completed the mission.

George's bodyguards had him trapped like a rat. Animal pressed his back to the bar, and kept his gun ready. At any moment he expected the gunners to come over and try and finish him, but he had something for them when they did. When a few seconds passed without him being swooped in on, he spared a careful glance over the top of the bar. He was just in time to see George and his crew making their way down the steps. If they made it to the main area, it was over. There was no way they'd be able to take them in such a thick crowd.

Animal bounded over the bar and gave chase. The sour bodyguard lumbered down the stairs, knocking people out of his way, while the second one protected George. His legs were shaky and it looked like he would pitch over at any minute, but he held tight to his gun. As soon as Animal made to take a step down, the third bodyguard, opened fire on him.

"I show you my hospitalities and this is how you do me?!" the third bodyguard fired shot after shot at Animal. Thankfully he was drunk and a poor shot.

Animal popped up and returned fire. He hit the third bodyguard twice in the chest, sending him spilling over the railing and down to the main floor. While he had been busy with the third bodyguard, George and the remaining two were just reaching the main floor. There would be no way Animal could get to them in time. Thankfully, he wouldn't have to.

"You need some help, Blood?" Ashanti walked up on the sour faced bodyguard who was leading the pack. He jammed his gun under the bigger man's chin and pulled the trigger, and put his brains on the ceiling. Just as Animal had predicted, his friend was there when he needed him most.

The second bodyguard raised his gun, trying desperately to defend George and get them out alive, but his movements were sluggish and he had trouble collecting his thoughts. It took a great bit of effort, but he was finally able to point the gun at Animal. "Don't come any closer," he slurred.

Animal's dark eyes drank him in. Even with the gun, he knew the bodyguard was frightened. "You can have the long walk," Animal nodded to the exit, "or the long kiss," he brandished his gun. "Pick your poison."

The second bodyguard knew it was a hopeless situation, but he'd rather take his chances against the killers rather than having to go back and tell Lilith he had let something happen to her baby boy. Either road he took would've lead to his death, but at least with the young man he would've died quickly. Lilith would draw it out, making sure he suffered. "Fuck it," he said and took a shot at Animal.

Animal moved just as the bullet sailed past his ear, nicking his face. Animal was fortunate because had it not been for the affects of the sedative, he'd have been dead. Animal fired on the move, striking the second bodyguard in the hip, sending him down and knocking the gun out of his hand. He ignored the pain in his hip and tried desperately to retrieve his weapon. His fingertips had just grazed the handle of the gun, when Animal's booted foot came down, breaking several bones in his hand. The second bodyguard howled in pain, clutching his hand. He rolled over onto his back and found himself looking up the barrel of Animal's gun.

"Let's hope you make better choices in your next life than

you did in this one," Animal told him before firing two shots into his face, ending him.

George found himself trapped between the two killers. He thought about attempting to bribe them, but from the looks of the two young men, this wasn't about money. They were killers. George didn't know either man and had no idea what they wanted with him, but he was willing to bet that it had something to do with his mother. George loved his mother dearly, but had no taste for the lifestyle she had condemned them to, which is why he put distance between himself and his family whenever he could. All he wanted to do was drink, smoke, count money and sleep with beautiful women. He was not a gangster, but always wound up guilty by association. Things were looking grim for George, until an angel of mercy intervened.

Animal felt the blow before he actually saw who had thrown it. A fist slammed into his chin so hard that his teeth rattled, and his eyes watered. When his vision cleared, he found a five-foot five obstacle standing between him and George. She was a petite looking young girl, but with the force of the punch she'd hit Animal with, it was obvious that she was no lightweight. She was dressed in a simple blue jumpsuit and flat shoes. Long black dreads spilled around her face and shoulders, while over-sized dark sunglasses covered most of her face. She danced on the balls of her feet like a boxer, thick lips pulled back in a sneer, challenging Animal.

Animal snarled, "Okay, bitch. I got what you need."

When Animal went to raise his gun, the girl slapped the back of his hand, causing the gun to go off and a slug hit the floor between her legs. She grabbed his wrist in one hand and the gun in the other, and twisted slightly, dislodging the barrel of the gun from the stock and tossing it away. She followed up by slapping Animal twice across the face, before shoving him back with a palm to the chest. She took a defensive stance, fingers bared like claws, waiting for Animal to make his next move.

Animal was caught off guard by the skilled attack. The girl was good, he had to give her that. But he was no slouch either. Animal faked high and went low, slamming his fist into the girl's rib cage. He regretted it when his knuckles made contact with whatever she was wearing under her jump suit. It was like punching steel. She leapt into the air and locked her legs around Animal's waist, while wrapping one arm around his neck. While holding onto him for dear life, she delivered elbow after elbow to his head, attempting to knock him out.

"Bitch, get off my homie," Ashanti grabbed the girl by her dreads and pulled her off Animal. Normally he wouldn't have put his hands on a woman, but they didn't have time to be chivalrous about it. With all the ruckus they'd caused it'd only be a matter of minutes before the police responded and were on the scene. It'd be best if they were gone by the time that happened.

The girl spun like a helicopter, breaking Ashanti's hold. She threw a punch, which to her surprise he blocked, and followed with one of his own, knocking her sunglasses off. She came back with a kick to Ashanti's ribs, and when he went to block it, she found an opening. She grabbed his wrist and turned it until the point where she heard it crack, and relieved him of his gun. She viciously stomped the back of Ashanti's leg, dropping him to one knee. She placed the gun to Ashanti's skull and forced his head up so that she was looking him in the eyes.

She wanted to see the moment of his death, as she did with all her victims. When their eyes locked it was as if someone had thrown a bucket of cold water on her. It was impossible.

Something heavy slammed into the girl's back, knocking her across the room and sending her crashing into a table. The force of the impact knocked the gun loose from her hand. She looked up and saw that Animal had regained his second wind, and was picking up the gun. She spared Ashanti one last glance before hurling a chair at Animal. Animal covered his face against the chair, and that split second he'd taken his eyes off the girl was all that she needed to vanish.

"You good?" Animal helped Ashanti to his feet.

"I think so," Ashanti checked himself over. "Where's George?"

"He made a run for it during the fight. If we hurry up, we might be able to catch him before he makes it too far," Animal started towards the fire exit, but no sooner than he had gotten to it, it came bursting open and several uniformed officers came rushing in. they quickly surrounded Animal and Ashanti with their guns drawn.

"Drop the guns and let me see your hands," a red faced officer with a buzz cut pointed his gun at Animal.

"Don't make me tell you again," the officer reinforced. His hand gripped his gun tightly, looking for a reason to discharge his weapon.

Ashanti looked like he wanted to go for it, but a look from Animal told him to stand down and do as the police ordered. There were only four of them, but Animal was sure there was a small army of blue soldiers not far behind them. Even if they weren't outgunned, these were still cops. To kill a street nigga carried a heavy sentence, but to murder a law enforcement agent carried the needle. Reluctantly, Animal tossed his gun to the ground and got on his knees, and Ashanti reluctantly did the same.

Kneeling, Animal and Ashanti gave each other dumbfounded looks. For all the crimes they had committed in the streets, all the years of dirt they'd gotten away with, it seemed like poetic justice that they would get knocked off for trying to do something good. Animal thought of the wife he would never see again and the kids he would never get a chance to know and it made his heart heavy. In his head he could hear Gucci's voice warning him not to go, but he didn't listen. His damnable sense of nobility had fucked him once again. Animal thought about all the things he had overcome in life, just to go out like this. Another street nigga caught with his hand in the cookie jar.

Animal was numb as the officers placed handcuffs on him. He had promised himself a long time ago that he would never feel the uncomfortable touch of the silver bracelets ever again, but here he was. He cast a glance over at Ashanti, whose face wore a look of utter disappointment. He was a young man, and would never get to grow to be an old one . . . at least not on the streets. True to his word, he had given his life for Animal.

As the cop was pulling Animal to his feet by his arm, he told him, "This is a fine mess you boys have gotten yourself into," he looked around at the damaged property and dead bodies. "You're going to prison for a long time behind this," he said proudly.

"Not on my watch," someone called out.

Animal hit the floor just before the first bullet ripped through the cop's face. Abel stalked across the room, firing both his .22 and the forgotten gun of one of the bodyguards. His face was twisted into a mask of hatred, and his eyes cold. The police tried to return fire, but he was relentless in his press. After seeing two of theirs go down, the other two retreated, screaming into their radios for back up.

"My nigga, right on time as always," Ashanti said proudly. Abel didn't respond, he just stood there with a dumbstruck expression on his face. "Abel?"

"They saw my face," Abel said, as if the realization of what he had done just set in. "I killed a cop and they saw my face. I'm going to the chair for this."

"Nobody is going to the chair. I'm going to get you all out of this, I promise," Animal assured him.

"You damn well better, since it was you who got us into it," Abel shot back.

Even if Animal wanted to argue the point, he couldn't because Abel was right. He had gotten them all into it, and it would be up to him to get them out. He wasn't yet sure how, but if there was a way, he would find it.

"Man, y'all can argue this shit later. For now, let's get the fuck outta here before we're all sporting new jewelry," Ashanti motioned to the handcuff hanging from his wrist.

Animal, Ashanti and Abel made hurried steps through the kitchen and out the back door. When they got outside they took off running for the avenue to meet Cain and Sonja. When they came out the mouth of the alley, they expected to find their comrades waiting, but instead they found nothing. The Denali was nowhere to be found. Police cars were coming onto the block from all directions, swooping in on the club. Nobody had noticed Animal and his crew yet, but it wouldn't be long before someone pointed them out. Soon the block would be shut down and there'd be no escape.

"Where the fuck are they?" Animal looked around frantically.

George stumbled out of the club, breathing like he had just run a marathon. It was two whole blocks before he felt comfortable enough to slow down. He had barely escaped with his life, which was more than he could say for his bodyguards. He had gotten used to the trio and they would be hard to replace, but not as hard to replace as he would've been. George wasn't sure what kind of shit his mother had gotten him into and he didn't intend to stick around and find out.

Family Business Protocol dictated George get to one of the safe houses and report immediately to his brother, but he was too rattled to bother with protocol. George wasn't even going back to his hotel to get his clothes; he was hopping in a taxi to the airport and getting on the next available flight out of New York. Once he was safely in the taxi he would call home and find out from his mother exactly what she had gotten him into this time.

George risked venturing out onto the avenue to try and flag a taxi. When he spotted a car that looked like it was slowing down, he began waving his hand frantically. When he got closer he realized that it wasn't a taxi, but an SUV. He was leery, but knew that in New York regular cars were also used as taxis, they were called Gypsy cabs. He would've preferred a yellow cab, but a gypsy would do. So long as he could get to the airport.

As George neared the vehicle, he squinted, trying to see inside. Through the car's high beams, he could make out two people in the front seat. He wasn't a native New Yorker, but George knew that cab drivers didn't usually ride two-deep, not even gypsy cabs.

The warning bell went off in George's head just as the driver stepped on the gas. George took off running as the Denali barreled down on him. He tried running on the sidewalk, hoping that it would deter the driver, but it didn't. The Denali jumped the curb and slammed into George, sending him flying through the window of a delicatessen.

While they were waiting for Animal and the others, Cain spotted George trying to get out of Dodge. He expected to see his comrades on George's heels, but when they never surfaced he figured something was wrong. He and Sonja debated as to whether to follow George or wait for Animal and the others. They eventually opted to go after George and double back when they'd gotten him under wraps.

Cain hopped out of the car and walked causally around to the curb. He stepped through the broken glass and sat George up. George seemed to be dazed so Cain slapped him a few time until he was lucid. "Can you walk?"

"I think my leg is broken, man," George clutched his ruined leg. It was bent at a very uncomfortable looking angle.

"Then hobble on your good one," Cain pulled him to his feet, and draped George's arm around his shoulder for support, while he half dragged him to the car. People looked on in shock as Cain stuffed him into the back of the Denali, and proceeded to bind his wrists and ankles with duct tape. Cain seemed not to notice them.

"Please, you gotta take me to a hospital," George pleaded. In addition to his leg being broke, he felt like the truck had caved all his ribs in.

Cain leaned in to whisper to George. "If my brother doesn't come out of that place in one piece the only place you'll be going is hell. I don't give a fuck who your mama is or whose kid she's trying to kidnap. If something has happened to my family, you're meat," he slammed the back of the truck shut.

"You fucking idiot, why did you hit him with the car? You could've killed him and we need him alive," Sonja barked once Cain was back behind the wheel.

Cain shrugged. "I could've killed him, but he's still breathing, ain't he?"

Sonja shook her head. "I swear, fucking with you street niggas is gonna get me and my baby killed."

Cain turned his eyes to her. "It's us *street niggas* that are the only thing keeping you and that kid alive, and we're doing it for free. If I were you, I'd try being a little more thankful and less of a bitch. Now let's get back to the spot so we can find out what the hell is going on with our people," he told her, putting the car in gear and pulling out into traffic as if nothing had happened.

Animal and the others decided that ride or not, they were getting the hell away from the crime scene, so they took off on foot. Animal and Ashanti drew more than their share of attention, running through midtown with handcuffs on. People screamed and pointed at the fugitives.

One brave soul tried to play hero, tackling little Ashanti to the ground and trying to hold him until the police arrived. It would cost him dearly. Abel walked up behind the man as he and Ashanti struggled, and blew his brains out in front of a few dozen witnesses. It didn't matter to him at that point. After what he'd done in the club, he'd be a hunted man for all his day and he seriously doubted the police would give him the benefit of a fair trail after killing two of their own.

The gunshots attracted the attention of two beat-walkers who happened to be across the street. "Stop . . . police!" one of them screamed. Abel responded by sending a hail of bullets at them.

"Let's go!" Abel barked, helping Ashanti to his feet.

The three of them took off running, with the police hot on their heels. It seemed like every block they passed, more people joined the chase. Soon they had a mob of police and citizens behind them. They had crossed 59th street and were heading for Central Park. If they could make it, they still had a chance to loose them under the cover of the dark park, but this was not to be. A police cruiser cut off their path, and two officers spilled out with their guns drawn. Between the cruiser and the mob, they were trapped.

Abel checked his gun and realized he only had a few bullets left. "Shit," he cursed. "I can't go to prison, man. I'd rather swallow one of these bullets than let them take me down," he said seriously.

None of them had any illusions as to what would happen to them if they were taken into custody. With Animal's record, they would throw him into the deepest, darkest hole they could find, if they didn't kill him first. Anything was better than captivity, including death.

There was the screeching of car tires, before the Denali

appeared seemingly out of thin air and rammed the police cruiser. One of the officers had been nearly cut in half when he got caught between the Denali and the door of the cruiser.

"Looks like you boys are in need of a ride," Sonja smiled from the passenger window.

"Sonja, I could kiss you," Animal said happily.

"Kiss me after I get these muthafuckas off our backs," Sonja told him, leveling the Mac 11. The machine gun roared to life, spitting hot death to anyone unfortunate enough to get in its path. This bought Animal, Ashanti and Abel a few precious seconds to jump into the truck. They hadn't even had a chance to close the doors before Cain peeled off into the night.

"Man, we thought y'all had split on us," Ashanti said, once they were far away from the park. They were currently on the FDR heading back to Brooklyn.

"Unlike some people, I'd never abandon my family," Cain said, half joking.

"Cain, I'm so happy to be alive that I'm gonna let you get that one off," Ashanti told him.

"What the hell happened in there?" Sonja asked.

"Things went to the left," Animal told her.

"Obviously," Sonja looked at the handcuffs he and Ashanti were sporting.

"We lost George," Animal said in a defeated tone.

"We know, and it's a good thing we found him," Sonja motioned towards the rear of the Denali.

Animal peeked over the rear row, and saw George's prone form, beaten, and bloodied with his hands and feet bound with duct tape. He got nervous, thinking George was dead, until he heard a faint moaning coming from him. "What the fuck happened to him?"

"Genius here hit him with the truck," Sonja motioned towards Cain.

"Stupid, just fucking stupid," Animal cursed. "If he dies we lose our leverage."

"Then I guess you just better make sure he doesn't," Cain said over his shoulder.

Animal just shook his head. Part of him wanted to sock Cain in the mouth, but there was also the part of him that understood. He had been Cain at one time, a young, angry kid who thought violence was the answer to all his problems. Speaking of answers, it had just occurred to Animal that he never had a chance to call Kahllah back and see what she wanted. If there had been a problem at home, he was sure Gucci would've called. She was still mad at him, but if there was an emergency she would've let him know. Whatever it was that Kahllah wanted would have to keep until they had George safely under wraps.

# TWENTY

GETTING THE BARTENDER TO GIVE UP THE waitress's address was like pulling teeth . . . literally. She started with his incisors, yanking them out one at a time with a pair of dirty pliers she'd found behind the bar. By the time she got to his cuspids, the bartender was singing like Jennifer Hudson when she was still fat. He not only gave her the waitress's name and address, but he spilled everything he knew about Panama Black.

According to the legend, Panama Black had come to America sometime around 2002, smuggled in on an ocean freighter amongst several other dozen refugees who had been sold on the idea that America was the land of the free. When they got here they realized that the freedoms promised by this country did not extend to those who had not been born on U.S. soil. Instead of equal opportunity, they found low wage jobs and harsh treatment. Some of the refugees who had come over with Panama Black accepted what they were given to work with and tried to make the best of it, but not Panama Black. He had not travelled from one end of the world to the other to become a dishwasher or laborer.

Panama ended up settling in a low-income neighborhood in Panama City, FL, where he took to the streets, doing anything and everything he could to survive. He was an ambitious young moan with the heart of a warrior. When one of the local gangs tried to make him a victim he made them hospital patients. He eventually developed a reputation as a tough guy in the neighborhood, and became popular with other young men his age. Panama would always preach to them how they were meant to be more than what their parents had settled for and that instead of sitting around waiting for a hand-out, they needed to take what the country refused to give them. Panama was a man on a mission, singlehandedly robbing American owned establishments and shaking down tourists. No matter what profited, he would always take a little to do things for the kids in the neighborhood, like buying them ice cream on hot days, or helping their parents buy food when things got tough. Panama was not only talking the talk, he was walking the walk. It didn't take long before some of the men from the families he was helping rallied to his cause. Panama went from a low level gangster to the voice of the people in his neighborhood, thus the legend of Panama Black was born.

It was Panama Black's sudden migration to California that had Kahllah puzzled. From what she understood, he had been content all these years to occupy his little section of Florida, so it came as a surprise when word got out that he was in California. The local crews buckled down and prepared themselves for a war they were sure was coming, but Panama never made a move on any of them. Outside of buying up a few properties in different ghettos in Los Angeles County and the occasional heist here and there, Panama Black had been relatively quiet since he'd been on the West Coast, at least that's the way it looked on the surface. If he was tied to Khan's coup, then there was something bigger going on than what was on the surface, and Kahllah intended to find out exactly what it was.

The girl he was seeing, Delores, stayed in seedy section of Watts. If not for the men posted up in front of run down houses, flying their gang colors, all you had to do was read the graffiti on the walls to know where you were. It was a warning sign to all outsiders.

Kahllah parked her car at the end of the street where Delores lived and killed the engine. She pulled out a pair of binoculars and surveyed the area. Delores's house sat at the end of a cul-de-sac, where it stuck out like a sore thumb. Whereas the houses around it weren't in the best condition, Delores's place was well kept. It was a two-story house, with a manicured lawn and paved driveway. She didn't see any cars in the driveway, but there was a light on in the living room so she knew someone was home. Whether she would find Panama Black inside the house was anyone's guess, but it was where the trail had led her.

This time, Kahllah wasn't taking any chances. She was dressed in fatigues and body armor. Strapped to her was her trusty harness, holding two pistols and several blades, but she had also brought some insurance with her, in the form of a shotgun, the same one the bartender had tried to use on her. She liberated it from him before she left and called it *compensation*. Kahllah preferred her blades to guns, but she had been ambushed twice in the past twenty-four hours and wasn't looking to let it happen a third time.

Slipping on her mask, Kahllah moved through the shadows, approaching Delores's house. As she neared it, she could hear shouting coming from inside. One was a man's the voice, and the other, Delores's, she presumed. She couldn't make out what they were saying, but they weren't seeing eye-to-eye on something. Kahllah crept into their front yard, making sure to stay low. She had almost reached the house when she noticed that the light upstairs had gone off, and the house was suddenly very quiet. She had a bad feeling, but she had come too far to turn back. If the answers she needed were inside that house, then no one short of God was going to stop her from going in.

Kahllah scrambled on all fours around the back of the house to where she found a door leading into the kitchen. She removed her lock-pick kit from her harness and within seconds had gained entry to the house. The kitchen, like the rest of the house, was dark. Kahllah hit a button on the side of her mask, and the eyeholes became night vision lenses. She surveyed the kitchen, with its dishes stacked in the sink and a pot still on the stove boiling. It appeared someone had left in a hurry.

She peered down the hallway that led into the living room and noticed that the television was on. Cradling her shotgun, Kahllah crept into the living room. She expected to find it empty, but to her surprise there was someone sitting on the couch, in front of the T.V. The cherry from the cigar he was puffing, burned ever so bright every time he inhaled. It was dark, so she couldn't see his face, but she could see the silhouette of his block shaped jaw and a head full of matted dread locks in the glare of the television.

When the cigar smoking man spoke, his voice was gravely

and had a thick accent. "You should've listened to the bartender when he told you that you didn't want to find me."

The light suddenly flicked on and off repeatedly and Kahllah found herself blinded. Next Kahllah felt two hits: something that felt like a bat crashing into the side of her head and her face hitting the floor.

"I told you not to do this shit in my house," Kahllah heard a woman saying. She was still laying face down on the ground, with her head ringing.

"What the fuck was I supposed to do? He came looking for me," the gravely voiced man shot back. "Look, just get your ass out of here. Me and the boys will clean this shit up."

"You better, because I'm not trying to lose my Section 8 over some shit you got going on. I should've never let your ass stay here."

While the two of them argued back and forth, Kahllah managed to push herself to one knee. Inside her mask she felt blood dripping down the side of her face from where whatever she'd been hit with had opened her up. She would likely need stitches and an entire bottle of aspirin, but those would have to wait. She could see her shotgun, lying a few feet away from her. She tried to lift her head, and found that it started swimming when she did. It would take a minute to pass . . . a minute she likely didn't have.

"Take our masked friend out back and put a bullet in his head, then meet me at the other spot. There's been a change of plans," the gravely voice man said to someone, who was out of Kahllah's line of vision. She could feel people around her.

"You got it, Panama," one of them replied.

It was him! Panama Black had been identified and that

was all Kahllah needed to hear. She felt the hands of two men take her about the arms. She allowed them to get her to her feet, before she made her move. Kahllah tapped her thumb against her index finger twice, and there was sound of air being released. Before the man holding her even knew what was going on, she was driving one of her retractable elbow daggers into his forearm. Moving fluidly, she swung him around into his partner, sending them both flying into the corner. Before either of them could right themselves, Kahllah was on her feet and had retrieved her shotgun.

"No wait . . . " one of them tried to plead, but she couldn't hear them over the roar of the shotgun. Kahllah spun, looking to Panama Black and caught the backs of his feet as he was fleeing up the stairs. When she went to give chase, Delores leapt into her back.

"You leave my man alone!" Delores screeched, trying to claw at Kahllah's eyes through her mask. She managed to tear the mask loose and dug her nails into Kahllah's exposed face.

Kahllah didn't have time for games. She grabbed Delores by both arms and broke her chokehold. While still holding her immobile by the arms, Kahllah threw her head back, slamming it into Delores's face. She then twisted one of Delores's arms behind her back and dislocated her shoulder. Kahllah looked at the girl rolling around on the floor, squirming and bleeding. All the fight she had in her was officially gone. With Delores out of the way, Kahllah went in pursuit of Panama Black.

She took the steps two at a time, chasing the elusive Panama Black. She lost her footing when she made it to the last step and stumbled backward, which is probably what saved her life. A chunk of the wall just above her tore away in a spray of plaster.

"You wanted Panama Black, well you found him. Now come see about him, muthafucka," Panama Black roared, firing off another round with his police issued Sig Saur 550. He was backing down the hallway towards one of his bedrooms.

Kahllah popped up, and fired a burst from the shotgun. She narrowly missed Panama Black as he dove into one of the bedrooms and kicked the door closed behind him. Kahllah moved swiftly down the hall after him. No sooner had she reached for the doorknob than the bottom of the door exploded, nearly missing her legs.

"You come on in here if you think your balls are big enough, but I'd best this Sig against your shotgun any day. I got enough bullets in here to last me until you get tired of waiting or the police come and lock us both up," Panama Black yelled through the door.

As much as Kahllah hated to admit it, Panama Black had a point. There was no telling how much ammo he had in the room with him and with all the noise the police were sure to be on their way, so there wasn't enough time to try and find another angle to get to him, but there was more than one way to skin a cat. Kahllah reached into one of the pockets of her fatigue pants and removed the gift Ashanti had gotten her for her last birthday. It was a shiny black grenade. If she couldn't wait him out, she would *flush* him out. Kahllah tossed the grenade through the hole in the door and ran downstairs to wait for the inevitable.

Kahllah had just made it out of the house, when she heard the scream, followed by an explosion. She ran around the back just in time to see Panama Black hit the ground with a thud. From the force of impact, she gathered that he'd very likely broken an ankle, possibly both, but it was better than getting blown to bits.

Though he was down, he was still not out of the fight. He was crawling across the grass, trying to retrieve the machine gun that had landed a few feet away. Kahllah dropped the shotgun and retrieved one of her pistols. She shot Panama Black in the back of one leg, then the other, immobilizing him.

"If you're gonna kill me then get it the fuck over with," Panama grunted against the pain. He was lying on his stomach, clawing at the grass.

"Not so fast, my friend," Kahllah stood over him. "I have every intention of killing you, but not before I have the answers I have come for." Kahllah rolled him over onto his back so she could finally look into the face of the elusive Panama Black, the man she had gone through so much to track down. When their eyes met, they both had the same slack jawed expression on their faces.

"YOU!" they blurted out simultaneously.

Kahllah whipped in and out of traffic, casting the occasional glance over her shoulder at her passenger, who was lying across the back seat, bleeding all over the place. Every time she hit a bump, he winced in pain, but he wouldn't cry out. He was too much of a trooper to show weakness in front of a woman. He'd been a chauvinist when they met and the years hadn't done much to change that.

On the streets he was known as Panama Black, but she knew him as Guillermo Petti. She had first met him years prior while doing a story on an El Salvadorian girl who had been wrongly imprisoned. She had been the girlfriend of a drug dealer who was under investigation by the DEA. The boyfriend knew he was hot, so he got the girl to unknowingly drive a kilo of cocaine across state lines for him. The police picked the girl up and charged her with the drugs. Even though they weren't hers, she took the charge for her boyfriend thinking she would get a lesser sentence as a first time offender, but they threw the book at her. After her incarceration, the boyfriend had abandoned her. Everybody in the neighborhood knew who the drugs belonged to, but despite them telling this to the police they kept the girl in custody and refused to go after the boyfriend.

Guillermo had been one of the biggest advocates for the girl, sighting the fact that the only reason they were holding her and not going after the boyfriend was because he was white and she was Hispanic. He was half right about that. Kahllah had done some digging into the boyfriend and found out he was the nephew of a councilman in Miami. He was protected from the law, but not from the Black Lotus. It didn't take much convincing for the boyfriend to come forward and take the weight. Thanks to Kahllah's article, the case had made national news and shed light on the epidemic of poor Latina women being used as drug mules. Guillermo was grateful for her help and promised that if he could ever returned the favor he would.

"So help me to understand how you're tied into all this," Kahllah told him.

"Look, it's like I was saying at the house, I've been doing freelance work for the Brotherhood for about a year or so now," Panama Black began. "It started out as small stuff, extractions, information gathering, raising hell . . . whatever they needed at the time. About three months ago they approached me with a business opportunity that I couldn't pass up."

"Which was?"

"The keys to the city in exchange for agreeing to help take out one of their own when the time came. On my life, I didn't know it would be you. Shit, as far as I knew, you were a reporter. I would've never pegged you for an assassin," Panama told her.

"There's a lot you'd have never pegged me as. Now tell me about this *keys to the city* business. What does that mean?"

"I was told that me and my crew would be given the start-up capital to relocate to California and build a criminal empire. We could get as many bricks as we could move for less than fifty percent of the going rate, on the condition that we only set up in Black Neighborhoods."

"All this is over drugs?" Kahllah was surprised. "This doesn't make sense. Kahn has always bent the rules of the Brotherhood to the point of almost breaking them, but he hates drugs. I couldn't see him giving you the green light to flood California. You better shoot straight with me or I'll drop your ass off on one of these corners to bleed to death instead of taking you to the hospital."

"I'm telling you the truth Kahllah. It was Kahn who first hired us to do the freelance work, but it was another member who approached us with the plan about the drugs in exchange for the execution."

This was an interesting twist. "Which member?"

"Kahllah, you know how y'all do it, no real names and no faces. I do know it was a female."

Kahllah stopped the car. There were only three women in

the Brotherhood, including her. One of the women was no lon-ger active and the other one had been killed in the line of duty a few years after Kahllah came into the fold.

"What are you doing? I need to get to a hospital," Panama told her. He'd already lost the feeling in his legs and felt himself going into shock.

"I ain't taking your lying wet-back ass nowhere. Here I am, trying to be amicable about this and you want to continue to lie. I'm the only female member of the Brotherhood. Get your lying ass the fuck out of my car," she leaned over and pushed the back door open.

"Kahllah, either we're talking about two different organiza-tions or someone isn't keeping you abreast of new members. On my kids, I'm telling you the truth. I met her once, but didn't see her face because she was wearing a mask, but she was definitely Brotherhood. All her credentials were in order. She even had a funny flower carved into her mask like the one on your knife," he pointed to the dagger hanging from Kahllah's harness. In the hilt was carved her calling card, a Black Lotus flower.

Kahllah's mouth suddenly became very dry. She pointed her gun at Panama. "What kind of flower was it? And if I think you're lying, on my life and my order, I'm going to kill you right here."

"I don't know, it was some kind of crazy looking flower," Panama said nervously, holding his hands up to shield his face from the gun.

"Then that's too bad for your ass," she cocked the hammer.

"Little Flower!" He blurted out.

Kahllah felt an icy chill go down her spine at the phrase. "What did you just say?"

"Little Flower," he repeated. "I don't know the broad's name who commissioned me, but there was another female member there who I heard her call Little Flower. You hear the name before?"

"Yes . . . many years ago."


Kahllah had been an initiate to the Brotherhood, barely sixteen years old. Priest had been her sponsor into the order, but once in she would learn a specialty field from different members. Her weapons instructor had been Tiger Lily. She was a cruel and hard woman with a no nonsense attitude. None of the initiates liked her because she was so mean, but she was arguably the best any of them had ever seen using an edged weapon.

One day Kahllah had been in class, clowning with one of the boys during Tiger Lily's lesson. For disrupting her class, she decided to make an example of Kahllah.

"Since you obviously know enough not to need my instruction, why don't you come up here and help me with this demonstration for the rest of the class, Little Flower," Tiger Lily challenged her. Little Flower was a nickname Tiger Lily used with all the prospective female members of the Brotherhood. It was deemed that all women who took the oath would be named after flowers, to remind them that they were little more than pretty things, and not forged of the same steel as the men. There had been five prospects in Kahllah's initial class, but she was the only one who lasted more than a month.

Cockily, Kahllah got up and went to the front of the class. She grabbed one of the wooden swords from the barrel that held them, ready to show off her superior swordplay skills.

"Little Flower, you're good with a sword, better than most of your classmates, but those are not what we'll be using for today's demonstration," Tiger Lily informed her, to Kahllah's surprise. Tiger Lily picked up two devices Kahllah had seen before, but never used. They were hand straps, with claw-like blades protruding from the knuckles. They were called Tiger Claws.

"But I've never used them before," Kahllah said.

"No worry, you're such an expert I'm sure you'll catch on quick enough," Tiger Lily smirked, fastening the claws to her hands. "Meet me in the center," she told Kahllah and walked to the middle of the room, where the students had formed a circle.

Kahllah was not skilled in using the Tiger Claws, swords were her area of expertise, but she couldn't let Tiger Lily embarrass her. Strapping the claws on, she went to face her instructor. The fight was over in less than a minute. Tiger Lily had cut her up so bad with the claws that Kahllah had required stitches.

Tiger Lily was there while the medics attended Kahllah's wound. She was a general bitch any other time, but she was looking at Kahllah almost passionately. "Little Flower," she began, "I know I hurt your pride, but it was a necessary evil. The lessons we learn about death are only a small part of what makes us so efficient. We must also learn humility, which is the lesson I have taught you here today. Each enemy is to be approached with same preparation, no matter how big or small. To underestimate your enemies is to offer yourself up for death. Do you understand, Little Flower?"

"Yes, mistress," Kahllah said just to shut her up. It wouldn't be until years later that she was really able to digest the lesson Tiger Lily had taught her that day, but it would be the last time she ever underestimated any of her foes.

Kahllah's head felt like it was spinning from the new development. So far she had a coup going on in the Brotherhood and a ghost who had come back to life to become a cocaine distributor. It was something straight out of a movie.

"Panama, I have one more question and this is an important one, so think very hard before you answer," Kahllah told him seriously. "This person from the Brotherhood, who offered you the cocaine deal, did she happen to mention where the drugs would be coming from?"

Panama Black thought on it. "Come to think of it, she didn't. Honestly, it wasn't my business. So long as we got to eat, the coke could've come from the moon for all I care. One thing I do remember though was that she spoke Spanish fluently."

That was the last piece of the puzzle Kahllah needed. Initially, none of it made sense but when she looked at the timeline of events the pieces started coming together. The attempt on her life . . . Red Sonja's sudden appearance to enlist Animal in her schemes . . . on the surface it seemed coincidental, but Kahllah didn't believe in coincides. Animal was not only going against Poppito, but the Brotherhood as well. Everyone was in grave danger. Kahllah stepped on the gas and the car shot out like a bullet.

"What are you doing? The hospital was back there," Panama Black pointed out, looking at the emergency sign that was now behind them.

"Your legs are going to have to wait. I have to warn my family," Kahllah said, steering with one hand and dialing her cell phone with the other. She tried Animal first, but he sent her to voice mail. She tried him four more times with the same results. "Shit," she cursed, punching the dashboard. Her fool of a brother was likely walking himself into certain death and she couldn't even warn him. She tired another number, and waited, praying that she picked up.

# TWENTY-ONE

INSTEAD OF GOING BACK TO CAIN AND ABEL'S apartment he drove them to an isolated section of Brooklyn, where they kept a large storage unit. Cain had an arrangement with the people who owed the facility, so they never disturbed his storage unit. This is the place they had chosen to execute the next phase of their plan. "He don't look so good," Ashanti said, looking down at George, who was stretched out on a blanket. His breathing had become shallow, and he was bleeding from the mouth.

"You wouldn't look so good either if somebody hit you with a truck, would you?" Sonja asked sarcastically. She was kneeling beside George, examining him. In addition to being a kingpin's daughter and trained killer, Sonja was also a registered nurse. She hadn't practiced much medicine since she had come to work for her father, but she was their only option for getting George medical attention because they couldn't very well take him to a hospital.

"How is he?" Animal asked.

222

"Alive, but I don't know how long that will hold true if we don't get him to a hospital to see a *real* doctor," Sonja replied.

"We both know that's out of the question. Patch him up as best you can and get him ready for our presentation," Animal told her. He then turned his attention to Ashanti. "Let me holla at you right quick, Blood," he led him from the storage unit and out of earshot of everyone else.

"What's up?" Ashanti asked.

"What was that all about at the club?" Animal asked, getting straight to the point.

"What do you mean?" Ashanti faked ignorance.

"Don't play with me, Ashanti, because I ain't got the head for games right now. I'm talking about that business with shorty with the dreads. That girl wasn't no street rat trying to save George, she was a trained killer. She could've popped your head off, but she didn't. She froze when she realized who you were, like y'all knew each other. Something you wanna tell me?"

Ashanti lowered his eyes. "No . . . , I mean yes . . . shit I don't know, Animal. I think I might be going crazy."

"Why don't you tell me what the deal is and let me be the judge of your sanity," Animal said.

"I can't say for sure, but I think that was Angela," Ashanti said.

"Your sister? I thought she was dead?"

"So did everybody," Ashanti said. "You know for years we looked for Angela. When I got my weight up, I even hired an investigator of my own to try and find her. The only lead he was ever able to find is when the dudes who ran off with her were found at the scene of a mass slaughter somewhere in Illinois. After that I assumed she was dead too and just stopped looking."

This threw Animal for a loop because it was the first time Ashanti had ever confided in him that he continued looking for Angela when everyone else had given up. "Ashanti, are you sure that was Angela?"

"To be honest, no. I haven't seen Angela since we were little. It looked like it could be her, but I can't say for sure until I see her again," Ashanti told him.

Things weren't adding up to Animal. If by some long-shot the girl at the club was Ashanti's estranged sister, how did she tie into Sonja's people in Puerto Rico? The rabbit hole continued getting deeper and deeper.

"Fella, y'all might want to hear this," Cain called out to them. Animal and Ashanti went back into the storage unit to find Cain, Abel and Red Sonja huddled around Cain's cell phone, which was on speakerphone.

"Are you all listening?" A female's voice came over the speaker.

"Who is it?" Animal asked.

"Her," Sonja said in disgust.

Animal immediately knew she meant Lilith. "How did she get your number?" he asked Cain.

"That's what I'd like to know," Cain cast a distrustful glance at Sonja.

"Don't go racking your brains about how I was able to contact you. Just know that my reach is endless," Lilith said. "So, you have allied yourselves with the traitorous whore Red Sonja, and made her problems your problems."

"Wouldn't be no problems if you weren't trying to kidnap my daughter," Animal said.

Lilith laughed. "Is that what she told you to get you to throw your life away? Dear boy, I was lead to believe you were smart, but obviously, I was misinformed. I can't say that I fault you. Sonja can be quite manipulative when she puts her mind to it."

"So says the baby snatcher," Sonja capped.

"Shut your lying mouth, Sonja. I could push a button and have your lives all ended without having to leave my house if I so chose, so show the proper respect," Lilith spat.

"What do you want?" Animal asked.

"You have sought to hurt me by taking my son, but George is a soldier. He knows the risks that come with being a part of this family and is more than prepared to die to protect us, if need be. How many of you can say the same?"

"What are you getting at?" Animal didn't like where the conversation was going.

"It's very simple. You've taken something from me and I in turn will take something from you," Lilith said wickedly.

Sonja snorted. "Is that supposed to be some kind of threat?"

"No, that is a fact, but here is the threat; if my son is not returned to me in a timely manner and in perfect health, I am not the only mother who will weep for her child," she told them and ended the call.

"What the hell did she mean by that?" Abel asked the unspoken question.

The answer to the question hit Animal like a bag of bricks. "T.J. and Celeste!" he gasped.

When Gucci got out of the shower she heard her phone ringing. She ignored it, and continued drying herself and then started applying lotion to her legs. She had been having a rough few days and didn't feel like talking to anyone.

No sooner had her phone stopped ringing, than it started again. Frustrated, Gucci reached for her phone, ready to curse out whoever was blowing it up, when she heard the doorbell ringing. "If it ain't one thing, it's another," she slipped on her robe. Scooping her cell phone off the table she went to answer the door.

T.J. and Celeste were in their favorite spot, sitting in front of the television, when Gucci passed through the living room. T.J. was so engrossed in the television program that he didn't give Gucci a second look, but Celeste did. She had a worried expression her face.

Whoever was ringing the doorbell had started banging on it, heavily, irritating Gucci. "I'm coming damn it, hold on!" she shouted. In her hand, her phone began ringing again. She continued to ignore it until she saw Kahllah's number on the caller I.D. "Hey sis," Gucci cradled the phone to her ear.

"Gucci, thank God. Is everything okay?" Kahllah asked frantically.

"Yes, everything is fine. Are you okay?" Gucci asked nervously. She had never heard Kahllah sound so rattled.

The banging on the front door continued.

"Gucci, I need you to gather up the kids and get them out of the house, now!" Kahllah warned her, but the warning came too late.

On the other end of the phone, Kahllah could hear the sound of the door being kicked in, followed by screaming and gunfire.

"Gucci . . . Gucci, are you there? What's happening?"

Kahllah asked in a panicked tone. A few seconds later the line went dead.

Gucci was frozen in terror as men dressed in all black and carrying assault rifles stormed her house. The one leading the pack was a well-built Hispanic with a bald head. On the sides of his skull Gucci saw two devil horns tattooed. Her moment of frozen terror was broken up when she heard T.J. screaming. Her eyes shot across the room and she saw two of the black clad men trying to take T.J. and Celeste. Gucci's parental instincts kicked in and she went immediately into survival mode.

Gucci made a mad dash for the couch, trying to retrieve the shotgun Animal kept hidden underneath it. Her fingers had just grazed the butt, when someone grabbed her by her hair and dragged her back. It was the man with the tattooed head. He motioned to one of his men, who looked under the couch and came up holding the shotgun.

The man with the tattoos shook his head in disappointment. "When I came, I had intended on treating you with the respect due a woman, but since you want to act like a bitch, I'll treat you like one," he punched Gucci in the face, dropping her.

Gucci lay on the ground, head spinning and jaw throbbing. She had been hit in the face by a man before, but never with that much force. Part of her wanted to just lie on the floor rather than risk getting hit again, but she remembered the kids. She had to save them. Gucci faked like she was still stunned, while the tattooed man sent one of his minions to get her up. When he was right on top of her, she kicked him in the nuts as hard as she could.

Gucci scrambled for dear life, across the living room floor

towards the kitchen. She got up and rolled across the counter, just as a hail of gunfire hit it. Dishes shattered and splinters of wood came away from the cabinets, eventually dislodging one and almost dropping it on Gucci's head.

"Finish her, and let's go," she heard the tattooed man say.

Gucci could hear the heavy footfalls of boots, crossing her living room and getting ever closer to her. When they were right on the other side of the cabinet, Gucci popped up with her hand tucked inside a cereal box.

One of the men laughed. "What, do you plan on making me breakfast?"

"No, nigga, but you sure are about to be food!" Gucci pulled the trigger of the gun inside the cereal box. The bullet struck the man in black in the throat, knocking him backward. She ducked back behind the counter just as the remaining men returned fire. Gucci cowered behind the counter, trying her best not to get hit. She could hear the kids both crying, and it only added urgency for her need to get to them. Then just as suddenly as the shooting started, it stopped.

"Hey, little bitch. I want to show you something," she heard the man with the tattooed head shout.

Thinking it was a trick, Gucci remained where she was. That's when she heard T.J. cry out to her.

"Mommy, help!"

Gucci peeked around the counter and what she saw made her heart skip several beats. The man with the tattooed head was holding T.J. with a machete to his throat. Gucci sprang to her feet, gun drawn. "If you don't put my son down so help me I will—"

"You won't do shit but watch this ugly little fucker bleed

all over these expensive tiles, if you don't toss that gun away and play nice." The man with the tattoos on his head warned. Gucci still looked hesitant. "Oh, you must think I'm fucking around," he pressed the blade tighter to T.J.'s throat, causing him to scream.

"Okay, okay," Gucci tossed the gun and raised her hands in surrender. "Just don't hurt my baby."

The man with the tattooed head, passed T.J. to one of his minions and stalked towards Gucci. He grabbed her by her throat and lifted her off her feet, causing her robe to come open. His dark eyes took in her nude body beneath the expensive silk. "My orders were just to come here and collect the little girl, but I think I'm going to have some fun with you first."

# EPILOGUE

KAHLLAH JUMPED THE CURB AND KNOCKED OVER two bushes when she pulled up to the house. Panama Black was still in the backseat, bleeding and begging her to take him to the hospital. Kahllah ignored him, and jumped out of the car, making a mad dash for the house.

Both guns in hand, she approached the front door to find it ajar. "Gucci," she called out, but got no answer. She crept into the house and her heart leapt into her throat. Furniture was overturned, and the living room and kitchen were both riddled with bullet holes. Her mind went to the kids, and she ran upstairs to see if they were okay, but found no signs of them . . . she was too late.

Kahllah ran downstairs. If something had happened to Animal's family on her watch, she wouldn't be able to live with herself. She heard the sound of a ringing phone somewhere amongst the debris. It took her only a few seconds to find it, lying on the floor near the kitchen. When she bent down to pick it up she noticed the blood. "Hello," Kahllah answered, following the blood trail which lead to the other side of the kitchen counter.

"Kahllah? Why are you answering Gucci's phone?" Animal asked on the other end.

Kahllah heard the questions, but couldn't find her voice to answer him. What she found in the kitchen stole her breath and broke her heart.

"Kahllah, talk to me. Is everything okay?" Animal asked in a panicked tone. He had a feeling in his gut that something wasn't right.

Kahllah composed herself enough to finally answer her brother. "No, everything is not okay."

At Kahllah's feet lay Gucci's body. She was naked, and beaten so badly that Kahllah almost didn't recognize her. Blood still trickled from her throat where it had been slashed. True to her word, Lilith aka Tiger Lily would not be the only mother weeping for her child.

TO BE CONTINUED

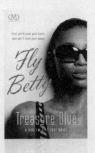

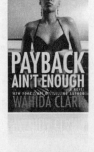